The Beast

The End Times Odyssey (Book 2)

Daniel Fulton

Pi-Writers Press

Pi-Writers Press Kokomo, Indiana

ISBN: 979-8-9865149-2-5 (Trade Paperback)
ISBN: 979-8-9865149-3-2 (eBook)

Scripture verses are quoted from the King James Version (KJV). Public domain.

Contents

1

Marriage Bliss

She heard his car pull in. His favorite meal was on the stove. He would be famished after his long train ride. Yussaf's business took him many places away from their upscale Damascus neighborhood, so she relished these intimate dinners. There was no football game on tonight so she would have his undivided attention. She greeted him at the door with a kiss.

"Hello love," she said with that look that drove him insane even after all these years.

"Hello darling!" he replied, sweeping her off her feet and onto his body, kissing her passionately.

This is what it's all about, he thought to himself as they walked arm in arm to the kitchen.

"I've cooked your favorite Kibbeh; you just have time to freshen up before its ready."

He kissed her lightly again and left to wash off the travel grime and get into the right frame of mind to enjoy the intimate dinner awaiting him. Marian was the best stress reliever in the world.

He was so lucky to have such a beautiful bride, he thought.

The demands of selling the newest high end Tesla self-drives to the elite clientele he catered to took him away from her too much.

He flashed back to his last sale. He rented (at his best client, the Saudi Prince's expense, of course) a very large helicopter to deliver the latest Tesla to an island the prince owned.

Every Villa the prince owned had to have its own Tesla, or two, or three. Good for his business, Yussaf thought, but he shook his head at the over-the-top opulent lifestyle the prince demanded while his subjects struggled.

He dismissed the thoughts and focused on the tantalizing aromas coming from the kitchen.

He entered the warmth of the kitchen filled with those wonderful smells and found her focusing on the last dish before she moved it to the dining room table. He slipped his arms around her waist from behind and gently kissed her neck. She turned and brushed her lips across his cheek and glided out of the room with the dish in her hands, beckoning him to follow with her body.

They savored the food and each other's company.

"How was your trip?" she asked.

He chuckled, "You remember the Saudi Prince I've talked about? Well, he bought another Tesla from me. I think that makes five this year! We had to deliver this one to an island in a helicopter! He didn't quibble about the price." He shook his head and savored another bite of her delicious Kibbeh. "How was your day?"

She nibbled at her food and smiled. "My sister and I went to the market early to pick up what we needed for the evening meals. She brought along her two-year-old twins. They were such a handful. They have changed so much since I last saw them. They are so precious."

Her look changed as she spoke. He sensed what was coming. The mood in the room changed. He raised the next bite to his lips, then put it back on the plate.

Here it comes, he thought. They seemed to have this conversation more often lately. She was fertile but he was almost sterile; the doctor's conclusion after every test they could run.

She wanted a baby so badly. They tried every natural fertility method known. They tried artificial insemination, in vitro fertilization; everything. Nothing modern medicine had to offer worked. Now she was pushing for an anonymous sperm donor. Her words always cut him like a knife. More than anything in the world he wanted to give her his baby. His brain threw these jumbled thoughts at him in a nonstop barrage. He felt like a failure.

He put his hand up in an effort to quell the coming argument. It didn't help. She started in.

"We could pick a donor that looked like you. Skin, hair, eye color, height, it would be just like you. See, it's all here in this brochure that I picked up at the fertility clinic. No one would have to know but you and me."

He sat stunned. She went without his knowledge to a sperm bank. He stared at the glossy advertisement. It was just like going to his dealership and picking out a car.

"It is a very simple procedure..."

She rattled on about the details but he wasn't listening. He rose, dropped the brochure on the table and threw his napkin on his plate; his appetite gone.

He walked out the door and past his car out onto the sidewalk, his hands thrust into his pockets, his shoulders hunched over in utter defeat. He wasn't angry with her. He was angry at life.

Why did I insist on going with my father on that mission trip to the Congo? He thought for the millionth time.

What was to be a two-week trip for him turned to an extended disaster. A luggage snafu at the airport in the capitol city of Kinshasa meant the hydroxychloroquine (Quinine tablets used for malaria) was lost with the luggage. The extra in his carryon luggage was stolen from his bag, along with his passport and some money. The fateful decision was made to go on without it. Surely the luggage would find its way to them soon.

He still remembered the oppressive humid heat and the swarming mosquitoes in the village they served. After three days the luggage hadn't arrived and he was feeling very weak, sweating profusely, and confused. *At least I remembered that much,* he thought.

He walked on, his mind replaying the experience.

I wish I could remember those two weeks, he thought but once again coming up empty.   High fever does that to the mind. He learned that first-hand.

Marian and he learned the devastating reason they hadn't conceived; another side effect of the high fever was sterility. He was almost completely sterile. The Doctors told him it was a common side effect of high fever but that it was temporary. A test six month later, when he should have been over the effects of the fever, revealed another problem. A genetic defect, not the high fever made him sterile.

The Doctors gave him a one-in-one-hundred-thousand chance of fathering a child.

He turned toward home. His profound sadness weighted his every step. He felt like he was laboring up a steep hill on level ground.

What a cruel twist of fate, he thought. He tried looking on the bright side.

At least they learned early on, not that there was anything he could do to alleviate the problem, he mused.

2

Making Up

She sat alone staring at the flickering candle. A kaleidoscope of colors and shapes danced through the tears welling in her eyes. She rose slowly, her sadness hindering her movements as she put the food she had prepared away.

When we go to the park or on a stroll, I see how he looks at the couples' pushing strollers and carrying toddlers in their arms, she thought.

She could see the longing in his eyes for a baby, just like her. She thought this time when she brought it up things would be different! He even brought up the subject of adoption once but she wasn't ready to give up on having her own baby.

She couldn't explain her obsession with having a child. It was bordering at times on irrational, given Yussaf's condition.

At least going on that ill-fated mission trip led to the knowledge of his condition. That was her Yussaf, she thought. He has a big loving heart and deep abiding faith to match and that was part of the problem.

He clung to the story of Abraham and Sarah in the bible. In their old age they were blessed with Isaac who went on to Father nations! Yussaf looked on his affliction as giving God an opportunity to work a miracle in his life. She was on board with his faith in the beginning, but her biological clock was ticking like the old Grandfather clock in the hall in the silence of night. Her faith in the miracle was diminished by age. Her obsession to have a child was beginning to cloud her judgement.

Marian slipped into her night clothes, her movements slow and deliberate, not wanting to climb into the lonesomeness of the empty bed. When she couldn't put it off any longer, she lifted the corner of the comforter and slid between the sheets, her body curled into a fetal position. Her pillow dampened with her tears.

Darkness greeted Yussaf when he returned. He fumbled with the lock and gently opened the door, entered slowly, and shut the door behind himself so the only sound was the latch clicking into place.

Marian heard him from the time the sensor activated the lock. It lit up her phone on the nightstand. She knew he would come back but she still said a prayer of thanks, and one of apology for her doubt.

He made his way slowly through the dim shadows cast by the late evening light. The dining room and kitchen had already forgotten about the day's events. He made his way to the bedroom in silence, shed his clothes, pulled back the covers, and slid in beside Mariam.

She feigned sleep as he settled in. He gently touched her shoulder.

"Marian, I'm......"

Before he finished "sorry" he was smothered with wet "I'm sorry" kisses, her arms flung around his neck. The sullen clouds left the room, swept away by the building unquenchable passion. They made love into the wee hours of the morning.

Maybe this will be the time, she thought as she positioned herself to receive him.

3

Immaculate Deception

Yussaf was again gone on business. She went about her daily routine with a lightness and joy she hadn't felt in a long time. She thought to herself, *I know this month will be different. I am already late for my period, and I'm usually like clockwork. I know it's too early to hope, but I've never been this late before.*

Each passing day more excitement crept into her psyche, but it was way too early to share with anyone. She breezed through her chores and decided to break for a cup of tea. She put the steaming tea on the table by the window where she liked to sit. She was two weeks late. Tomorrow she would get a pregnancy test to confirm her suspicions. She settled down with her tea.

That's when she felt the tug in her abdomen. *No! This is not happening!* She thought. She leaned on the table and sat motionless. *Maybe if she didn't move she could stop it,* she thought.

She knew that was irrational thinking. She closed her eyes and prayed.

She couldn't put it off any longer. She had to know. She moved to the bathroom. The red stained tissue in her hand told the harsh truth. She sat there staring in disbelief.

The Grandfather clock disturbed the silence and chimed three o'clock in the hallway. Silence again.

Seconds later a mourners wail again split the silence. It came from the depths of her soul and echoed through the house. She mourned for her lost happiness, the baby that might have been, and the bond she would never experience. She mourned for Yussaf and the child he would never have. She had experienced this disappointment every month of her married life, but this was the cruelest.

She came out of the bathroom dejected, to the table where her now cold tea waited. She sat staring into the dark liquid as if there was some miracle within. She heard the clock chime four times in the hall. The chimes, though not altered, sounded to her like the death knell at a maritime mass funeral.

In the minutes after the chimes, she rose and walked into the study. She sat at the computer and searched sperm donors.

The line was crossed. No more waiting, no more disappointment.

Yussaf didn't have to know.

She would be extra careful in choosing the donor and he would raise it as his own!

I'm taking this matter into my own hands, Marian decided.

The only thing that mattered to her now was conception.

Her clandestine online searching brought up many sperm banks and many doctors specializing in fertility, but they were far away, or required spousal consent. It was ironic, a single woman only had to prove stability and financial responsibility, but she needed the consent of her spouse.

Finally, she located a fertility clinic in a neighborhood not far from her in a part of the town she normally avoided. It was mainly Muslim; Christians were not welcome. She plotted in secrecy by saving from the generous allowance Yussaf gave her to run the household, squirreling away a little at a time to prepare for the day she would conceive.

She monitored her ovulation for months. In early April, Yussaf would be gone on a business trip. According to her calculations, her time would be right. She started birth control as instructed by the clinic months before the event. At their instruction she stopped the pills and got the hormone shots at the specified time.

When the time came for Yussaf to leave on his trip, she kissed him and saw him off. When he boarded the plane, she called the clinic on the special number they provided.

"Conception Therapy Clinic," the voice on the other line chimed. "How can I help you?"

"This is Marian Wassef. I was supposed to call when my time was right. I am ripe."

"Very well," the voice said. "Get here as soon as possible. We will be ready."

She returned to her car in the parking garage. The sleek new Tesla reminded her of a spaceship. When she touched the car with the palm of her hand the wing-like door opened. The seat swung outward to receive her body. When she sat down the seat moved back into the comfort position she had preprogrammed.

Her hands trembled as she entered the address in the computer. The satellite and the car communicated, and the soft hum of the electric drive whisked her away to her appointment with destiny. When she arrived, the nurse greeted her behind the receptionist desk.

After the preliminary identification and paperwork, the nurse escorted Marian to a large pristine room with a single hospital bed. Marian found it odd that every time she had been to the clinic, she was the only patient. She dismissed the thought, disrobed, and put on the hospital gown as instructed.

The nurse came in wheeling a cart with monitors and medical supplies.

"I'm going to give you a shot that will help the process succeed," she said. "The doctor will be in shortly."

Marion had reservations about taking a shot that wasn't mentioned in any of the procedures. Maybe she just missed it in her briefings. She let the excitement of the moment cloud her judgement.

Marian drifted into limbo. She thought of Yussaf making love to her and wanted to reach out to him and embrace him, but her arms wouldn't move. She was totally paralyzed. When she awoke, the nurse was in the room.

What is that acrid sulfur smell?" Miriam asked.

"I don't smell anything. Perhaps it's a mild reaction to the medicine we gave you. The procedure is finished. You need to rest and not move for a while to ensure the procedure's success. All we can do now is monitor you.

Later, still groggy from the shot, Marian sat on the edge of the bed. Gingerly she rose to her feet and tested her balance. When all was well, she dressed, combed her hair, and straightened her cloths in the bathroom mirror. She brought her palm against her lower abdomen in anticipation. She looked the same but she, for the first time since her false alarm, had hope (and science) on her side!

Marian paid the rest of the fees for the procedure and signed the final forms.

The nurse smiled at her and said, "Good Luck!"

"Thank you!" Marian beamed.

She walked into the bright sunshine, elated. Her self-drive car flawlessly delivered her home.

A cup of tea would be nice, she thought and busied herself with the task.

As she enjoyed the tea, the lingering effects of the shot dissipated. Her elation waned as the adrenalin left and the heaviness of fatigue settled. Yussaf's flight wouldn't arrive until tomorrow afternoon, so she crawled into bed.

As the sheets caressed her body, she drew into a fetal position. She touched the bed where Yussaf usually lay and wished he were there to comfort her. She was experiencing soreness in her groin and lower abdomen that dampened her elation. This was something they didn't warn her about in the briefings. She felt violated. Tomorrow, she would leave early to pick up Yussaf at the airport and stop by the clinic. She had questions.

The next morning, the sun demanded her attention. The morning shower felt comforting as the warm water caressed her body.

"I wonder why I am so sore today?" she said out loud.

Nothing was said about that in the briefings, she thought. *I'll leave early to pick up Yussaf and stop by the clinic.*

She stepped out of the shower and dressed. She fumbled in her bag for her phone and dialed the number.

"This is not a working number. Please check the number and dial again," said the emotionless computer-generated voice on the other end.

She carefully dialed again. Same result.

She would just stop by; she still had the address.

The car pulled to the curb at the pre-programmed address. The clinic was gone! The building was boarded up, and a "For Lease" sign hung in the storefront window.

What had she done? What had they done and why? Desperation panic filled her thoughts. Her quest for motherhood had clouded her judgment and good sense. The web of deceit she wove threatened to smother her.

4

Punishing Pregnancy

Doctors ordered Marian on bedrest for the last two months due to her difficult pregnancy. In the last few days, her blood pressure shot up, and the protein in her urine landed Marian in the hospital. She was only 36 weeks, but her gestational diabetes made the fetus grow too large for her petite frame. Marian insisted they give the baby as much time as possible for the lungs to develop, but finally it was time.

The labor pains were mild and infrequent at first. Two hours after the first pain she noticed a little more intensity in the contractions. Yussaf, who was by her side, timed the contractions and confirmed they were getting more frequent.

The nurse came in to check on her dilation. Another contraction started while she was there. She reassured Marian, and especially Yussaf that every-thing was progressing normally.

I feel so helpless, he thought. Another contraction.

Marian was now breathing deeply; part of the technique they had learned in birthing class.

The last five hours have been stressful for me, I can't imagine what she feels, thought Yussaf,

He didn't leave her side, or let go of her hand. He dabbed her forehead with a cold towel between contractions. He laid his head on her bed just to rest his eyes. He must have dozed off because he jumped like a bolt of lightning struck him when the next contraction hit. Guttural moaning escaped her lips.

"Two minutes, Marian! They're two minutes apart." The words tumbled out of his mouth in a mixture of excitement and concern.

The nurse came in to check on Marian again. The pads under were wet. Her water broke.

Yussaf almost knocked her over in his exuberance to tell her, "Two minutes, they are two minutes apart!"

She moved back from him and nodded. She never told the fathers that the monitors gave them all that information continually. It gave the fathers a sense of purpose. Some figured it out, but most were clueless.

At twelve hours the doctor came in to talk to the couple.

"Marian, Yussaf, the dilation progress has stopped. Marian, your vital signs are troublesome.

The stress of being bedfast for so long is a factor so in my opinion we should consider taking the baby cesarean section. We talked about this option for your situation."

"No, no, no!" Marian protested' "give me more time!"

She had more to say but the next contraction cut her dialog short.

Yussaf looked on in wild-eyed bewilderment thinking, *I don't know what to say. I can't stand to see Marian suffer much longer.*

"Give...me...more...time, doctor!"

The good Doctor never understood the reason some women felt they had to endure so much pain. An epidural could ease her suffering and the outcome would be the same but so far, she had refused.

"Ok, but we will be monitoring you closely. The first sign of trauma to you or the baby and we'll go in and get that stubborn child!"

He grinned at her. Her eyes said "Thank You" and again the pain started.

He chuckled, kissed her hand and marveled at her courage and stamina.

Marian desperately wanted to experience childbirth, but her birth canal wasn't large enough to accommodate the man-child she was birthing. Twelve more hours she endured the intense pain until the doctor ordered the C-section. This time Marian didn't put up a fight. The nurse put something in the IV, and the pain diminished to a menstrual cramp.

She was aware of being whisked into the operating room. Yussaf held her hand as they rushed headlong into their future.

The doors to the operating room opened wide for all who were sterile to enter. Yussaf was left behind in anguish. The doctors were ready. Marian was readied. The incision was made.

Dr. Habib was a veteran of many C-sections but he had never seen, or smelled, anything like this. The newborn was the size of a small toddler, beautiful and perfectly formed—a full head of hair, dark eyes, and a great set of lungs! After handing the infant over to the nurses, he had to step back. The smell of burning sulfur gagged him. As a surgeon, he thought he had smelled every smell the human body produced, but he had never smelled this. He regained his composure and examined the womb to finish his job. The uterus had the consistency of tanned leather. Her ovaries were atrophied and dead. She was barren. He would have to perform a total hysterectomy to ensure her survival.

• • •

Marian had many sleepless nights worrying about the events surrounding conception. When she did sleep, the recurring nightmare of lying paralyzed in the hospital bed at the clinic haunted her. The brimstone smell brought back those fears, but the scream of her new baby boy made it all worthwhile. She had waited so long for this moment to arrive.

After what seemed to be an eternity, the nurse placed her newborn son on her chest. She could not describe this moment in time by mere words. In all of human experience, only birth mothers are privy to this special bond. All the anxiety, all of the pain and suffering melted away.

Dr. Habib allowed Marian this moment before he had to deliver the bad news.

When the baby was taken to the nursery, he approached her. The years taught him to be blunt about these things so he laid it out, "Marian, I have some bad news."

"Is my baby all right?" she asked in a panic.

"Your baby is fine. It's you I'm concerned about. Your ovaries are full of cancer and your uterus was destroyed by the large infant. We had to literally cut it off of him. We have stopped the bleeding but it needs to come out also. There were places on it that I suspect is the start of cancerous tumors. It was not pliable like a normal uterus should be."

"What would cause that?"

"I don't know why for sure, but probably a genetic issue triggered by your medical issues carrying the baby. They will need to be removed immediately to ensure that the cancer doesn't spread."

"So, I don't have a choice?" she asked through angry tears. She had been through so much to get this far. No one except her knew just how much.

"The doctor put his hand on her shoulder and said soft but firm while looking her in the eye, "No Marian you don't. The alternative would be death."

He hesitated briefly to see if she had any questions. She was silent, staring into space, her elation at finally having her baby tempered by his news.

"Do what you have to do to save my life so I can enjoy the baby I sacrificed so much for," she answered.

While the nurses prepared Marian for surgery the Doctor sought out Yussaf.

"Congratulations, Yussaf. You have a healthy son. He weighs in at 7.5 kilograms and is sixty-six and six tenths' centimeters long. He is the largest baby I have ever had the privilege to deliver!"

Yussaf grabbed the doctor's hand and shook it vigorously, beaming with pride. This was one of Dr. Habib's favorite parts of his job. He loved the reaction of the proud fathers, especially the ones that could not witness the birth first hand.

"How is my Marian?"

"She came through the cesarean well, but there are complications we must discuss," the doctor informed him, still grasping Yussaf's hand.

He looked Yussaf in the eye and delivered the bitter news, "She needs a total hysterectomy immediately. Her whole reproductive system is involved. I'm afraid of the cancer metastasizing. We will have to remove everything for her to survive."

Yussaf's firm handshake wilted and he staggered from the news. Dr. Habib steadied him and put his left hand on Yussaf's shoulder to offer strength.

"You can hold your son while we work on your wife. The operation is routine and she is a fighter. She will be fine," the doctor reassured.

Yussaf walked to the nursery where he was instructed how to handle his newborn son. He was overwhelmed as he sat holding him. He was struck by how heavy he was and how long. His olive skin was perfect, and his eyes shone like black diamonds. Yussaf marveled at his strength and the size of his hands as he held Yussaf's finger. Yussaf envisioned the child as a leader uniting the world in peace. He smiled.

"Welcome, Nicholas Susej Wassef," he said softly as he nestled him in his arms.

That was the name Marian and he had agreed upon. After seeing his son for the first time, he knew they had picked the right name.

A nurse came for the baby and told Yussaf his wife was doing well. In a few minutes, he could go sit with her in the recovery room.

"We have a beautiful son," he said to her when she stirred.

"I know!" He looks like you," she lied.

She would tell Yussaf of her deceit when the time was right, on his deathbed, or hers. Now she just needed rest and his love.

5

The Formative Years

Nicholas grew fast. His schooling had to be specialized because he soaked up everything instantly and became easily bored. The teachers marveled at his natural leadership and his academic abilities, but on more than one occasion, he took over the class to the point the teachers were fearful for their lives.

Normal, well-behaved children seemed to come under his control and do his bidding. He could get a whole classroom of otherwise well-behaved children to terrorize their teachers and destroy a classroom while standing in the corner laughing with glee. The teachers could not control him. The children couldn't resist him; he terrified both of them.

His parents had no choice. They removed him from the education system and hired special tutors.

By the age of twelve, he could read in any language. He studied the history behind the Torah, the Koran, and the Bible. He was a scholar of politics and the different forms of government through history. He marveled at how easy the Jews were led astray, and how the Muslims could follow an illiterate prophet who had to use a scholar to write down the Koran. He wondered how the God of the Bible could let his son die on a cross. He wondered why Jesus, who had great power and could raise the dead, didn't unite the world under his rule.

Nicholas didn't believe in anything but himself and the power he felt within.

Nicholas knew that he was destined for greatness. He had recurring dreams of standing on a platform with people screaming his name and bowing before him. He needed to burst forth on the world stage.

An astute student of the human psyche, he observed that members of the public could not name their government representatives, or the local police chiefs, but they knew every statistic of their favorite football team. The posters of the players of the local teams were everywhere in his house too. His father was a huge fan of football and took Nicholas to every home match of the Egyptian national team, the Pharaohs.

Because of his size and speed, none of the neighborhood kids would play with him. They played for fun, he played for blood. He was much better than anyone else in the neighborhood and he knew it. They ran when they saw Nicholas.

One day, he approached his father, Yussaf, about trying out for a local team that served as the talent pool for the Pharaohs. Yussaf knew many influential people in the soccer organization because of his business dealings and his love of the game. Yussaf made a phone call to his friend, Anibus Antoun, who was in charge of recruiting for the seventeen and under Pharaoh's football club.

They exchanged pleasantries and agreed to meet for tea on Thursday.

"Anibus, I have a raw recruit I would like you to meet. He is my son, Nicholas. He wants an opportunity to try out and join a proper club. We can discuss it over tea on Thursday. If you agree, I will bring him along."

"Yes, by all means bring him!" We're always looking for new talent, and I trust your judgment, Yussaf."

Nicholas got his tryout. The scouts were skeptical because of his age but were awestruck with his ball handling. And the fact that he didn't seem to tire, no matter what drill they put him through. He would start practicing with the club next month.

It was by some sort of providence that an apartment opened for the family just a few blocks from where he would practice with his new team. Yussaf packed up his family and migrated from Syria to

Cairo, Egypt, to give his Nicholas every chance to succeed.

It was up to Nicholas now. The path to his destiny would start with this first step. He took his soccer ball into the street in front of his new home and started kicking it down the sidewalk beside his street to a blind alley close by, where he could practice undisturbed. He wanted to hone his skills before practice later in the day. He kicked the ball toward the lamppost and it hit dead center so the ball came directly back to him. He caught it with the toe of his shoe, lifted it into the air, and balanced it on his forehead. He dribbled it into the air repeatedly and finally, with the slightest variance, caused the ball to bounce in front of him where he gave it a vicious kick into the ally.

The ball bounced off the wall with such force that it hit the opposite wall in midair. He grinned and ran into the alley to continue his practice. The alley had one entrance, so his mother repeatedly admonished him not to play there. It was a favorite ambush spot used by the Muslim "enforcers" roaming the city at will and imposing Islam.

He ran into the alley to retrieve his ball. He hesitated as he rounded the corner. A man stood in the middle of the alley holding his ball in one hand and an AK-LSR rifle, (the latest in laser rifle technology) in the other.

"Come here, boy," he commanded.

Nicholas complied.

"Is this yours?" he continued, holding the ball up with his fingers spread, giving the impression it was on a pedestal.

"Yes, give it to me," Nicholas retorted, showing absolutely no fear.

The man flicked his wrist and the ball bounced onto the pavement. His four minions started kicking it clumsily around the alley, laughing, insulting each other's miscues. The leader raised his hand and one of the minions retrieved the errant ball.

They surrounded Nicholas in anticipation. They knew that if he wasn't a professing Muslim, he soon would be a convert, or a bruised and bleeding infidel.

"Are you a follower of Islam?" the leader asked Nicholas, leaning in nose to nose, eye to eye, annoyed that this young man showed no fear.

"No! Give me the ball!" Nicholas screamed so loud and forceful it echoed in the alley. The veins in his neck stood out, and his face glowed red, rage welling inside.

The leader blinked, taken back by the boy's reply. He recovered quickly, flicked the ball to the side, and raised the butt of his weapon to strike Nicholas's head. He would teach this insolent infidel to respect for Islam and more importantly, him.

What happened next could only have been documented by a high-speed infrared camera. Nicholas grabbed the leader by the throat, knocked the weapon out of his hands with his elbow, and threw him against the alley wall. Before he could fall to the ground, Nicholas caught him again by the throat and pinned him against the wall. The man's eyes opened wide, and fear permeated every pore. Nicholas drank in the delicious essence. He trembled like an addict reaching his high. He had never experienced such power.

The four minions stood motionless, paralyzed. The camera would have seen demons that left Nicholas the moment he grabbed their leader and documented the spirits as they entered the men. They were aware of Nicholas taunting, playing with the man they followed, like a cat playing with a mouse. They heard their leader beg for his life, whimpering a prayer to Allah. They desperately wanted to run but couldn't.

When the essence of fear started to wane and Nicholas got tired of the game, he slid his fingers around the man's neck at the base of his skull and placed his thumbs under the chin, causing the screams from his victim to become muffled grunts that might escape a castrated pig.

He lifted the man off the ground and with a violent snap, bent his head back, like opening a Pez dispenser. The body fell in a heap, convulsing and twitching in the throes of death.

He turned to the four. He could see the fear rising from their bodies like heat does in the hot desert sun. One by one, he dispatched them. The demons that paralyzed them returned to his body full of the essence of the fear he craved.

He dragged the lifeless bodies together side by side, facing east. With his powerful hands, he dislocated each jaw and thrust the weapons they carried down their lifeless throats, barrels first.

His last act was to pose them as if they were on their prayer mats facing east, praying in their mosque, thus defiling Islam, Mohammed, and Allah. He retrieved his soccer ball and bounced it on the pavement, catching it under his arm, and calmly walked out of the alley. He didn't want to be late to his first practice.

6

Karma or Coincidence?

Marian sat staring out the window from her hospital bed. *My life didn't turn out anything like I had planned. I couldn't even breast feed my baby without supplementing my milk with formula and goat's milk. He was just too much boy to handle. I remember just how sore he made me when he suckled.* She thought as a smile crossed her lips.

She touched the sore hard knot on her breast from the most recent biopsy and looked down once again at the tear-stained paper with the cancer diagnosis. She was coming to terms with it.

I wish my health had been better when Nicholas was young. Chione took such good care of him. She seemed to be the only person that could control him. He was so disruptive in his classes. He had control over his classmates and his teachers were afraid of him. I don't know what I'd do without her. Marian's mind wondered back to his childhood.

I remember when she was hired. I still think she bore an uncanny resemblance to the nurse in the clinic where Nicholas was conceived. I know in my mind that she is that nurse. I don't even know how I know but I know. I just wasn't in any position to question her. Lyla Chione Nasari, a regal sounding name for a nanny.

Marian flashed back to that time in her life. She remembered the first conversation she had with Chione...

When Yussaf left for work on Chione's first day and they were alone, she asked, "Were you ever a nurse?"

"No. Why would you ask me such a thing?" Chione lied.

"You look like a nurse I met in a clinic many years ago, before Nicholas was born."

"You must be mistaken," she lied while looking Marian right in the eye. "I have always been a nanny. Ask Yussaf. He did a thorough check on me."

The reconstructive facial surgery masked her other life from everyone, except Marian. Never had anyone questioned her about it. It had merely been an assignment. Wherever her master sent her, she was willing to go. She was just glad to be a part of his final plan. He gave her the wisdom to know Nicholas's destiny. She was not worried about Marian. Marian's own act of betrayal would keep her from pursuing the truth. Eventually, Chione knew she would gain her trust. It was in the plan.

Marian prayed constantly, but her prayers seemed to fall on deaf ears. She prayed for health, she prayed for Yussaf and Nicholas, and she prayed for her relationship with Yussaf to be restored.

Since her deception, she had become withdrawn and distant. Yussaf had the same love in his eyes when he approached her, the same tenderness in his touch, but she could not drink in the love she craved from him. She could not bear to gaze into his loving eyes.

It seemed there was a large camel in the room when they were alone. The camel's hot breath seared her neck in a constant reminder of what she had done. When she summoned the courage to confront her demons and confess, the camel would spit in her face and keep her weak and submissive with yet another health issue.

I know the only way I'll find peace is to tell Yussaf the truth. I vow I will, on his deathbed or mine, she thought as she hung her head in a coward's shame.

Since her hysterectomy, she had endured a prolapsed colon, gall bladder surgery, and liver issues brought on by the very difficult delivery attempt and the massive number of anti-depressants and pain killers she had consumed from the time she weaned Nicholas.

• • •

Marian was waiting for Yussaf to arrive so she could share the terrible news. She needed him desperately now. He had always been her rock. Even in her deceit. Her mind wondered again.

I can't believe my Nicholas will be fifteen in a few months. Yussaf and Chione have done such a good job with his soccer career. I wish my health had been better so I could be more involved. I'm so proud of him. I know he's caught up in his career but I hope he can come and visit me between games. Maybe when the Pharaohs play their next home game, he can come. She was still thinking back when Yussaf came into the room.

He hesitated at the door, steeling himself for what he might encounter. Marian never disturbed him at work unless something was really urgent. She rose from her chair as he entered. She collapsed in his arms, sobbing.

She looked up into his anguished eyes and said one word, "cancer."

They stood embraced, trying desperately to shut out the world and its cruel fate.

The doctor walked in.

"We have found a sizable lump in your left breast, Marian. I'm not sure why it didn't show up in any of the other breast exams you have had over the years."

"That fact alone disturbs me. That indicates this is a very aggressive cancer. The biopsy was not good. We will know more after testing but the cancer is extensive. We will remove the lymph nodes in the surrounding area and test them also. As we always try to do, we will do the least invasive methods first. Then we will follow up with chemotherapy.

Marian's knees buckled, so Yussaf helped her to the chair. He sat facing her, caressed both her hands to his cheek. He started rocking with grief, tears flowing down his cheeks.

The Doctor walked over to them and put her hands on their shoulders gently. She turned and left the room, tears leaking onto her cheek. This was by far the worst part of her job.

Yussaf was by Marian's side with every test. He held her hand as he always did. In a matter of hours, she would know her fate by the tests they were running on the lymph nodes they biopsied. When her surgical oncologist entered the room, she tensed in anticipation.

She greeted Yussaf with a handshake and acknowledged Marian.

"Marian, I'm afraid I have bad news. Judging from the lymph node tests, your cancer has spread through your body. We will need to do extensive testing. I'm afraid the prognosis is not good."

Marian's life became centered around hospital visits. Test after test confirmed the cancer doctor's suspicion. Weeks of testing left Marion depressed and weak. It seemed every test result came back worse than the last.

Finally, all the tests were run, all the results were in. Marian's cancer doctor called her in for a consult.

"Marian," she began, "After all the tests my colleagues and I agree the best treatment plan for you is a double radical mastectomy followed by chemotherapy treatments."

She watched Marian's reaction carefully. She knew that down through the years, Marian had suffered many health concerns since Nicholas came into her life. The Doctor wondered how much fight she had left. That was the most critical thing in any patient's recovery, their grit, determination, and strength.

Her reaction was classic.

"How much time do I have, Doctor?"

The doctor was evasive with her answer, "Each person is different. The answer to that question is up to you and God, Marian. I won't lie to you, the cancer in your body is extensive and will take aggressive chemotherapy. Your life is going to be very difficult for the next few months."

"What about quality of life? Will I be able to function and enjoy life with the treatment?" asked Marian.

Again, the doctor was evasive.

"That is entirely up to your body and your mindset. Your attitude and inner strength are critical to your healing." She answered.

"So, there is no other option other than surgery?" asked Marion.

The doctor took Marian's hand, looked her in the eye, and just said, "No."

Two weeks later, Marian entered the hospital. Yussaf was at her side as always. It was a somber ride in the elevator to the surgery center. Yussaf had a sinking feeling even as the elevator gently lifted them to the proper floor.

Again, he was left in the waiting room while his Marian was in surgery. An all too familiar place for him.

He paced slowly up and down the corridor, his eyes never far from the doors the surgeon would come through to tell him about his Marian. He fixed himself a cup of tea and drank it slowly while absently thumbing through the magazines on the stand between the chairs. The clock on the wall seemed frozen.

He sat directly in front of the doors, his senses tuned to the swish they made when they opened. His eyes closed involuntarily.

The doors moved and he jumped to his feet, eyes wide in anticipation. He could feel the rush of adrenalin coursing through his body even as his heart sank. It was an orderly taking a load of soiled linins to the laundry.

An eternity later, the doctor appeared. Yussaf rose and steeled himself for what she had to say.

"Marian came through the operation just fine. We removed a lot of muscle tissue and lymph nodes around the area. She is going to be extremely weak and in a lot of pain. Now the hardest part of her journey begins." "

"She will be out of recovery in about two hours. You can see her then but I suggest you don't stay long. She needs rest and so do you. I'll look in on her this evening."

"Thank God!" replied Yussaf.

The doctor wearily walked away massaging her neck from fatigue.

The weight of the world lifted from his shoulders. He had his Marian back. At least for now.

He called Nicholas to tell him the news.

7

Confession

Marian knew she would never get out of the hospital. The doctor's warning about the chemo's side effects rang true. She could feel her will lessen with every bout of nausea. Her body was tired of the fight.

"Please close the door," she said to Yussaf after the doctor left.

"I have a confession, Yussaf."

She thought of the vow she had made to tell him on her death bed, or his. That time was now. She hesitated, closed her eyes, and prayed for strength. The consequences of her deception might cause Yussaf to leave her alone in her final days on earth, but at least she could die in peace. He deserved the truth.

"Nicholas is not your son. "She blurted out.

Yussaf let go of her hand and stood abruptly. Marian was steeled for the furious firestorm from hell she knew was surely coming; the one she had envisioned in her mind every one of the thousands of times she had told him in her mind.

"I was not unfaithful to you, I was inseminated."

"Inseminated? But how...When...Why?

It hit him like a ton of bricks. Nicholas was not his child!

The hurt and betrayal welled in his eyes and spilled down his face. He could only stare, eyes unseeing through the tears. He ran out of the room down the hospital corridor, his forearm brushing the wall to stay balanced.

He staggered out of the hospital into the sunlight, down the sidewalk, out of the parking lot and into the street. He was angry that the pulse of the city flowed, uninterrupted, though his world had imploded.

He didn't know how long he walked; his mind filled with random disconnected thoughts. His exhausted anger allowed his body to collapse into a chair at a secluded table in the corner of a tea house.

He ordered a cup of tea. When it arrived, he caressed the cup with both hands, looking into the dark steaming tea, wishing that he could read tea leaves and know the future like the seers.

When his thoughts calmed, he faced the truth he had suspected for so long. At fourteen, Nicholas was a head taller than him, and his features didn't resemble his at all. He wanted to confront Marian, but it seemed that there was a bear in the room when they were alone, growling, baring its teeth, threatening to rip the flesh from his body when he thought of questioning his paternity. He was already sensitive about his inability to give her the baby she was so obsessed with. When the news of Nicholas came, he was elated but also troubled.

Marian lay alone in the hospital bed, IVs in her arm dripping with the only comfort she had left. She accepted the fact that Yussaf was gone from her life and Nicholas was caught up in his new career and had no time for her. At fourteen, he already had soccer scouts all over the world swooning. Even though her illnesses had taken normal motherhood from her, she was still proud of her Nicholas. She attended his matches when she had the strength, but mostly had to listen and watch from her bed.

A week passed. The chemotherapy made her violently ill, so she spent her days in a drug induced stupor. She was sitting in her bed surrounded by the bustle of orderlies cleaning and changing her bed when she glanced in the doorway. She blinked her eyes at the apparition, making sure it wasn't the drugs.

Yussaf paused to allow the orderlies to finish. When they left, he slowly walked to her bed and without hesitation gently embraced her. He felt her weak arms entangled with IV tubes around his neck, the intrusive heart beep of the machines monitoring her vital signs in his ears.

They stayed embraced until her arms could no longer hold him. As they slipped to her side, tears of joy washed her cheeks. Her shoulders straightened as the weight of her past lifted, and a smile appeared briefly across her lips. She would die in his comfort.

"I have someone here that needs to see you," Yussaf said through his tears.

The doorway darkened as Nicholas entered. He didn't have to duck his head to clear the doorway, but he was still growing. Two jackals with cameras, dressed as orderlies to slip by the nurse's station, seemed to fill the empty space around her and her son. She brought his large powerful hand to her cheek and wet it with her tears. The cameras flashed like a strobe light as the moment was being captured for his adoring public. He was there for a photo opportunity for his adoring fans.

Yussaf angrily chased the paparazzi out. He was concerned that the excitement would be too much for Marian.

She didn't care why Nicholas was there. All that mattered was that he came.

"Hello, mother," Nicholas said.

He took her frail hand in his large powerful one. He was appalled at her appearance. He was almost afraid to embrace her for fear of hurting her, but he bent low over her bed until their cheeks met. Marion raised her arms to embrace him.

"Do you remember the time I got in trouble in school for disrupting the class and they called you in to the Head Master, "Nicholas asked, trying to reconnect with his mother in a better time in their lives.

She chuckled, "Which time?"

He grinned and they moved back in time to his childhood.

"You were certainly a precocious child, and so smart!"

Nicholas blushed. Her and Chione were the only two people in the world that could control him and teach him anything. He didn't understand the feelings he had for her. She would do anything for him and he for her, but he couldn't, even with his great strength, do anything to ease her suffering now.

They spent the evening reminiscing about more innocent days before the demands of his public life came between them.

"Would you get me some water, Nicholas?"

He complied. When, in her weakened state, she dribbled the water onto her lips and chin, he gently dabbed it with a cloth. It occurred to him that their roles were reversed now. She used to do the same for him.

Yussaf looked on in approval. He couldn't remember the last time Nicholas came to visit his mother, even when she was in better health. He was glad he insisted.

Nicholas catered to his mother's every need while they talked; until she could no longer fight the pain medicines periodically coursed through her veins automatically, and drifted off.

Nicholas stood motionless over her, gently caressing her limp hand. He finally turned to go and caught the approving glance of his father. He was glad he came even though it was painful. He turned to leave, darkening the doorway with his departure.

His heavy footsteps echoed in the now deserted hospital corridor. Were those tears streaming down the cheek of the most ruthless soccer player to ever play the game?

Yussaf dosed off in the chair beside Marion's bed.

She stirred in the wee hours of the morning. Day and night meant nothing to her now. Yussaf touched her hand to let her know he was there. When the drug's hold eased, and she was fully awake she told her story.

She began, "I know it was fifteen years ago Yussaf but do you remember the last time we talked about artificial insemination? That night you stormed out of the house when I brought it up and later came back?"

She smiled weakly and squeezed his hand, "We made love into the wee hours of the morning like we did when we were very young."

A puzzled look came on his face as he searched his memory. There were so many memories like that between them. She saw in his face the delight when he remembered. He smiled the distant smile of past pleasures.

She continued, "I have never told this to anyone until now. My period was late that next month. I was sure I was pregnant, but it was too soon to tell anyone. I remember it like it was yesterday. It was two weeks into the next month, and I hadn't yet had a period. I was so happy! I breezed through my morning routine and fixed a cup of tea. I sat the tea on the table in front of my favorite chair when I felt the flow. I stood motionless, hoping against hope that my feeling was wrong, but it wasn't."

"I...I just snapped. The grief of all the disappointment for so many years followed by so much hope put me over the edge. I know it was wrong to do it behind your back. Can you ever forgive me?" she pleaded.

Yussaf was silent, contemplating what she had said. He should be furious with her, but her frail eyes looked at him pleading for forgiveness. He could never say no to his Marian.

"I should be mad at you, Marian, but your actions gave us Nicholas. Although I have always had my doubts that he was mine, I have raised him as though he was and will continue to do so. I don't condone your actions, but my stubbornness was a factor in your decision, so I will shoulder part of the blame with you."

He gently lifted her head slightly off the pillow and kissed her lips and wiped away her tears.

The pain pump sent the artificial sleep through her veins and she dosed off. Yussaf saw the peace on her face. A peace he hadn't shared with her for many years.

Marian died a week later. She had refused any further treatment. She wanted to go with a clear conscience. Yussaf held her hand during her last moment.

She died forgiven, not knowing the apocalyptic world events her deceit had helped unleash.

8

Soccer Domination

Nicholas played every soccer match with a vengeance. Even players in his own club feared him. If anyone missed an assignment or allowed the opposing team to score, he towered over them and growled in disapproval with the roar of a lion. No club he was affiliated with had ever lost a match. He moved through the ranks of Egyptian football at an unprecedented rate. By the age of sixteen, every major soccer club in the world was recruiting him.

Yussaf managed him well. He negotiated with many clubs but managed to convince the Pharaohs to sign him for the life of his career. He not only ensured Egypt the world cup for at least the next decade, but he also kept the opposition from stealing Nicholas. A dynasty was born.

The Pharaohs were unbeatable. Each win set an unbreakable record. They called him the Beast. Sportscasters all over the world used the name and the quote: Who is greater than the Beast? Who can play against him?!

Yussaf grew increasingly concerned about his stepson. Chione, Nicholas's nanny, teacher, and now promoter, seemed to have him scheduled for photo-ops or speaking engagements, promoting his career constantly. He no longer practiced with the club. He just arrived for the matches followed by his entourage of security people, keeping a space from him and his adoring fans and groupies.

Yussaf noticed Nicholas's eyes were bloodshot before the matches. He had the look and actions of someone on a drug-induced high. Yussaf and the league insisted on a drug test for Nicholas before every match to ensure the integrity of the league. Opponents accused him of being on performance-enhancing drugs every time he played.

Yussaf decided to find out the truth about the hours leading up to a match when the Beast disappeared.

He researched the latest camera drone technology.

Drone-Search Unlimited marketed a drone camera controlled by a chip placed discretely on the observed subject. It featured a lens capable of recording hundreds of square meters and software to allow focus on a single subject.

Yussaf planned his covert operation for weeks. He let no one in on his plan to minimize detection. He stayed away from Nicholas and Chione for fear that they might detect his intentions.

When he felt confident in his plan, he used his codes to gain access to the garage in the compound where Nicholas's fleet of security vehicles headquartered. The security routine involved vehicles leaving and arriving at various times to stymie the paparazzi and the groupies, who never knew which vehicle Nicholas was in. The tinted windows and security details were always secret. Not even Yussaf knew the schedule, so he placed an imperceptible piece of tape on the top of every vehicle that contained the control chip for each individual drone.

He stationed his control vehicle many blocks away and waited. As each car left the compound, the corresponding drone came to life and followed the car at a safe distance. He sat in his car and watched from a monitor.

Hours passed. Each car left and returned. Some circled the block and returned while others sought out gangs of armed men in places in Cairo famous for roaming bands of well-armed drug dealers and Muslim radicals, looking for infidels to convert to Islam.

The third car from the garage pulled up to the curb of a local militant hangout. The group of seven men was sitting around a table discussing the day's exploits when the long black limousine stopped.

Conversation halted as all attention turned to the limo. Out stepped a large, seemingly unarmed man who walked to their table and stood towering over the apparent leader.

"How can you allow that infidel football player called the Beast to defile Islam and your Muslim brothers on a daily basis?" the large man asked, waving his hand in a gesture of dismissal.

The fact that Nicholas was born into a Christian family and refused to convert to Islam was a sore point with the radical Muslims. They tolerated him because of the resulting glory the Pharaohs brought on their land.

The enemy of my enemy is my friend! The old Muslim saying excused the Islamic oversight, but it didn't quell the radical fire within those sworn to keep Islam pure and most holy in the eyes of Allah.

"Keepers of Islam?" the large man goaded. "Pathetic cowards, I say!"

Shuffling chairs and the sounds of seven weapons rattling to attention pierced the air as the men stood, surrounding the large man, guns drawn.

In the ensuing silence, the sounds of more guns echoed the first. The leader glanced at the long car. A gun stuck out of every slightly cracked window. Out of the sunroof, a large laser pulsed weapon instantly drew a beam painted on his forehead. All players froze.

The large man spoke, "It seems we are at a stand-off, warriors of Islam!" I think I have a solution to our dilemma if you allow me."

The leader nodded, never taking his eyes off the car.

"What if I told you I've been looking for a group such as you to talk to my friend, Nicholas, the Beast, into converting to Islam? He enjoys a lively discussion before he glorifies the Pharaohs in battle."

The leader didn't believe him. "Why would he come here? On the football field he is king, but out here he is just another infidel."

He prodded the man's chin with the barrel of his weapon.

A car identical to the first rolled to a stop. The door opened, and a large shadowy figure walked into the light of the café. The men recognized him instantly. It was the Beast.

"Let him go," the Beast commanded.

The leader hesitated for a second, analyzing the situation. He concluded that The Beast would be a great conversion, or at least a bounty. If he wouldn't convert, think of the ransom they could demand for him. He nodded at his men, and they allowed the large man to pass.

The large man looked up into the eyes of the Beast in a passing acknowledgment. He was already counting the bit-card bounty he'd just earned for supplying the pre-match festivities for his master.

He calmly walked to his limo and disappeared as the car sped away.

The seven turned their attention to the Beast. He strolled toward them as the guns trained on him.

"If Allah is so great, then why does he need riffraff like you to spread his message?" he said as he confronted the seven.

The Beast was trembling with the anticipation of an addict shoving the needle in his vein. The predictable pattern emerged. The leader raised the butt of his weapon as the demons did their job on the others. They looked on in a paralyzed fear. The Beast enjoyed the anticipated terror of the six, as he toyed with their comrade. They were allowed enough movement to see and capture in their minds the terror the Beast inflicted. He enjoyed fantasizing about what he could do to elicit the most fear and pain. He was marinating them in their misery.

He grabbed the man's wrist in his vice-like grip, rendering the man immobile. He placed the trigger finger of the man's hand between his thumb and forefinger and snapped it like a small twig. The man screamed in delicious agony as the pain set every nerve in his arm on fire on the way to his brain.

The Beast hesitated, drinking in the agony, until the screams subsided. Then he grabbed the next finger and repeated the act. He dragged the man around the circle of the six like a rag doll, making sure they all shared equally in his agony.

Yussaf watched on his computer screen in horror and disbelief. When the Beast's needs were satiated, he grabbed each man by the skull with one hand, like palming a soccer ball, looked him in the eyes, and snapped his neck. After finishing with the last man, he straightened his clothes and strolled back to the car.

Yussaf took control of the drone making it hover above the gruesome scene. He was in shock, unable to believe what he had just seen. As he watched, a truck covered with canvass pulled over to the curb. Two men dragged the corpses to the curb and dumped them into the truck. They climbed into the cab and lumbered away. He followed with his drone camera to an industrial furnace in the middle of a scrap iron yard used for melting down metal. One by one, they dropped the bodies into the furnace to be consumed by the intense fire.

A man walked into the dim light with a device that looked like an old cell phone. He wiped the evidence off all cameras and the vending machines in the shop and calmly disappeared.

Yussaf sat in his car motionless, his brain digesting what he just witnessed. He retrieved all of his drones and drove slowly home pondering his next move. He made copies of the camera files. He paced and prayed. Not since he lost Marian had he been so in need of God's help.

9

Pure Evil

Many sleepless nights passed for Yussaf. He still trembled at the memory of the callous pleasure Nicholas took in killing those men. Why did he need to do these heinous things?

Yussaf knew now that he had to work as diligently to stop Nicholas as he had done to ensure his success. These camera files needed to get into the hands of as many people as possible, but whom could he trust to expose this madness? Most of his Christian friends were too afraid to cry out in the name of Jesus for fear of persecution. They quietly practiced a watered-down version of the Word, but one of his friends remained a tireless warrior for Christ.

Markus Rashida had been beaten, thrown in prison, and branded as a zealot. No matter what they did to him, he thrived. He had a loyal but clandestine following that seemed to defy attempts by society to quiet their message. Yussaf knew Marcus would have the connections to get his message out. He sent the file to him with this message:

Greetings in Christ,

I have an urgent matter for your attention. Nicholas, my stepson, the one they nicknamed the Beast, is a Beast!

I cannot bring myself to write down the atrocities you will witness on the files. I need your help and expertise to expose him before he kills again.

The Pharaohs will be playing tomorrow night. While everyone is distracted with the match, meet me at our old meeting place for tea. Do not reply to this message. Just come!

Please! I beg you!

Your friend,

Yussaf

Yussaf and Markus met at the University of Cairo. Marcus was a Messianic Jew and Yussaf a Coptic Christian from Damascus attending on an academic scholarship. The two of them had many heated discussions about religious doctrines in the university café over tea. Sometimes it seemed that the only thing the two agreed on was that God was the Creator and his Son was sent to redeem them with his blood. Those were such innocent, passionate times.

Even then, Marcus was a scoundrel. Coptic Christians were a minority in Cairo, but the number of Messianic Jews in the whole city wouldn't fill a synagogue. Somehow, he managed to bend rules and get enrolled in school and thrive, always one step ahead of his persecutors.

Yussaf, on the other hand, just wanted to complete his business degree, get a good job, and lead a comfortable life of anonymity, raising a family. Now he seemed to be thrust unwittingly into this intrigue.

I hope Marcus remembers the good times as much as I do, thought Yussaf. He waited at the table that they shared with so many friends. Yussaf glanced at his watch frequently as he waited, wondering if his friend would even show.

Across the room walked a familiar figure. His face bore the deep wrinkles of a hard life. A scar born of his persecution ran down the right side of his face. Yussaf rose to greet him. They embraced and kissed on both cheeks. As they sat down, Yussaf noted the passion and fire remained in his friend's eyes.

They sat in silence while Marcus' tea was served, just relishing the renewal of the bond true friends share. The soccer match started on the large monitor at one end of the café. Marcus started reminiscing about old times but he could feel the discomfort in his friend.

One of the greatest pleasures in Yussaf's life, watching football, had been taken from him the night he witnessed his own stepson, whom he nurtured and raised, commit senseless atrocities.

When the commentator yelled the familiar, "Goooooaaaaalll!!!" into the microphone, Yussaf cringed. The memory of those men's skulls being handled like soccer balls exploded in his head.

"What do you think we should do, Markus?" he asked.

"We need to find out what his intentions are. If he is a psychopath that enjoys killing, then we need to expose him to the authorities and stop him."

"He needs to be stopped no matter what the reason!" Yussaf countered, his eyes wide with urgency.

"I agree, my friend, but I fear there is way more to this than mental illness. Think of the well-orchestrated events leading up to that scene. Many people were involved, and the operation was too smooth. This has been done many times."

Yussaf's stomach turned, and he felt ill with the truth he knew, but stifled within. He listened.

"I have had recurring nightmares about a ruler addressing a large crowd from a platform in a stadium. The crowd cheers and chants his name. He plucks the head off a white dove and thrusts it toward the crowd. The headless bird flies around until every drop of blood is spilled on the crowd. Wherever the blood lands on the flesh of the people, large sores emerge. They moan in agony but continue to worship the ruler. He raises his arms and the sufferers cheer. Then the stadium fills with what looks like blood and all are washed away. The evil of the ruler disturbs me so much I have lost sleep."

Yussaf listened intently at his friend's story. The vivid narration disturbed him.

"Could this be a prophecy?"

"I don't know, Yussaf, but we need to find out if these two nightmares are related. It is no coincidence that we have been brought back together here after all this time.

They finished their tea and walked out of the building. The match was still on the screen when they left, instilling a sense of urgency to their actions. They walked the same walkways they did as students.

Marcus was the first to speak. "We need to get close to Nicholas so we can learn his plans."

"Believe me, that won't be an easy task. I am the only one allowed past his security now. If anyone enters his complex to deliver anything, they are followed by armed guards until they leave. I am the only exception."

"We could plant a listening device in his office, but the questions we need answers for may never be discussed," Marcus said, thinking aloud. "What we really need is to confront him."

At the back of his mind, he knew the only way to learn what they needed to know was to send Yussaf in to ask the right questions with a recording device. It would be very dangerous, almost certainly deadly, if their suspicions were right. He couldn't ask anyone to risk their life in such a way.

Yussaf was deep in thought. He spoke calmly, as if a great burden had been lifted from his soul. "I will go in search of the truth. If our suspicions are correct, it won't matter; I have nothing left to live for. My wife is gone and my son turned out to be a beast. I am alone in this world, except for my Lord and Savior."

"I hope my premonitions are wrong, my friend."

The rest of their time was spent planning. Marcus had many contacts that could still get state-of-the-art technology without a lot of government red tape.

Yussaf went about his usual routine. His office was next to the living quarters of Chione and across the hall from the suite with "The Beast" emblazoned on the door. He was a manager in name only; his job was to keep league officials informed and happy by providing them with drug screenings and keeping Nicholas aware of rule changes. The only thing he did daily was to go through the mounds of endorsement proposals that Nicholas received and send the most lucrative ones on to Chione. She and Nicholas made the decisions now.

Yussaf met with Marcus and was briefed on the workings of the microphone and camera. It was one unit and looked exactly like the other button on Yussaf's Pharaohs jacket.

The time had come for the confrontation. Yussaf loaded his camera drone footage into the screen that Nicholas used to study game films. He entered the suite and sat down in the lounge to wait. Yussaf said a prayer.

A few minutes later, the Beast came in, still wearing his Pharaohs uniform. He was bantering with the security guards that followed him about the latest match. They kept vigil outside his door. Chione followed him. They were so caught up in the excitement of the match, which the Pharaohs won, they didn't notice Yussaf. When they acknowledged him, they fell momentarily silent.

"Hello, father," the Beast said with a smirk. "Did you catch the match? We won."

"Hello, son," Yussaf replied. He had never told Nicholas the truth behind his paternity.

Chione sensed something different in Yussaf.

He walked over to Nicholas's desk and clicked the remote. The big screen came to life with the horrifying events Yussaf had witnessed. Chione tensed.

"Ah, yes, I remember this one!" Nicholas said with glee. He went into a play-by-play narrative of the gruesome event, smiling.

"What is this?" Yussaf demanded.

Chione confronted Yussaf, "It's necessary. If he didn't feed his need for domination and fear by killing these insignificant mortals, every match would be a disaster of blood and death played out in front of his adoring public. The time will come when it will be used as a tool for world domination, but that time is not yet here."

Chione tensed and started to convulse. Out of her being came a reddish swirling mist that filled the upper third of the room.

Yussaf smelled brimstone and felt the sinister evil as Satan entered the cloud. He was paralyzed, but not with fear. A sense of calmness overtook him.

"Do you think your God will save you?" the voice of Satan spoke from the cloud. "Do you think I can be stopped? Your Book lies. I will be victorious with the help of my son with whom I am greatly pleased! Yes, Nicholas is my son!"

Nicholas had never heard those words, but he suspected no mortal could be his father.

"Yes, he is the anti-Christ!" the voice spoke again. "Look at his middle name. Didn't you see the irony in a mortal given name that spells Jesus when re-versed?"

The dark one continued, "Do you remember the story of Job? Your Creator allowed me to take every-thing from Job to get him to curse God, but I couldn't take his life. I have dominion over the earth. I can cause suffering; I can cause a man to kill his brother, to be a prisoner of greed and lust, but I could not kill.

"My son is half human. I can manipulate and dominate vicariously through him. Best of all, I can kill at will. I can feel the terror as I pluck the souls of men from this life and throw them into the depths of hell!

"When the people of the world gaze at me, they're repulsed and will not give themselves over uncon-ditionally, but by human standards, my son is beau-tiful. Together we will rule the world!"

The Beast rose and turned his attention to his earthly father. "You're my first Christian kill. I will savor my sweet victory."

Yussaf felt himself suspended in air by an invisible force that pulled at his chest but left his head, arms, and lower torso dangling. He hovered there helplessly as the Beast approached.

The Nicholas part of the Beast hesitated, putting a hand gently on his earthly father. The primal, evil part of the Beast roared.

"Kill him and bring me his soul!" the evil being in the room demanded.

The Beast grabbed Yussaf by the throat and lifted him so he could make eye contact. The Beast needed to see the terror, feel the fear, and drink in the smell of death. The Beast hesitated. All of the others he killed were insignificant to him.

This was different. He felt the conflict of good and evil for the first time in his own soul. He was puzzled by the emotions.

"Kill him!" the evil in the room roared.

Nicholas hesitated. His hand trembled as he dealt with his inner feelings.

"Kill him and bring me his head!" Satan insisted.

Nicholas felt the power of the darkness his father controlled. He didn't understand Satan's hold on him but he couldn't resist.

Yussaf gazed into the eyes of his stepson son for the last time. He felt a presence that lifted him, protecting him from the carnage. He watched as the Beast tortured his body. The Beast was enraged that Yussaf didn't show the fear he so craved. The Beast sniffed Yussaf like a wild animal, his rage peaking when he was denied his drug.

Yussaf watched from somewhere in the room, engulfed by the peaceful light, unaffected by what he saw. The Beast thrust his two middle fingers into Yussaf's throat just above the collar bone and ripped his head from the body. His body fell in a lifeless heap. The Beast held the head high and roared in triumph, puzzled by the absence of the fear.

The evil left their presence. The red mist returned to Chione, and she woke from her trance. Nicholas saw her true essence for the first time, a demon, a minion sent to do the will of Satan, his true father. He smiled, as it all became clear. His transformation into the darkness was complete. He stared at the lifeless heap in the room still puzzled, still craving more fear.

10

The Resistance

Marcus was beside himself. He could not believe what he was seeing on the monitor. He grabbed his head and rocked with grief as he wailed uncontrollably. He grieved for his friend and the glimpse into the future. He understood his recurring dream. He couldn't move from his chair; the death of his friend could not be unseen.

Yussaf was the first of the martyrs in the end times. Nicholas was the Beast, the ruler, the deceiver. The innocent blood shed would be avenged by God in the form of boils and sores on the people that allowed themselves to be deceived. The blood spilled would wash them all away into the abyss.

He wondered aimlessly for days, not knowing what to do. God had revealed to him the future of the world. Revelations spelled out in real time.

He found himself sitting at the table that he and Yussaf shared a short time ago. His hot tea arrived.

He caressed the cup, waiting for it to cool. Random thoughts collided in his mind, careening against one another, jostling for his attention.

A Bible verse flashed across his mind as if he was watching a monitor. "Let the unrighteous continue to be unrighteous, and the vile continue to be vile, let the righteous continue to practice righteousness, and the holy continue to be holy" (Revelations 22:11).

It came to him. The time of redemption was fast coming to an end. The people of the world soon would not seek repentance, led astray by the great deceiver.

He was totally spent, physically and mentally. He savored his tea, sipping it as if it was the only good thing in the world, his head bowed low, eyes closed in-between sips. His hand brushed across a paper lying on the table. He hadn't noticed it before.

It was smooth as glass and emblazoned with random shapes and colors. He ran his finger over the surface and a picture of his Lord and Savior appeared. He gently placed his hand on the image. A peaceful reassurance tingled in his chest. Suddenly, he was not alone. He felt the presence of many souls united in Christ even if he didn't see them.

He left the table and walked away. A vision of a place where he needed to be gave each step a sense of urgency. In a secluded part of the campus stood six people, talking, adamantly gesturing, asking the same questions he had.

As soon as he approached the group, a stairway appeared, and they walked into the pale light. The ramp closed and they found themselves in some sort of an aircraft. The pilot sat at a large monitor.

She swiveled around in her seat and instructed them to find a seat and buckle in for the flight. Her joyful demeanor and bright smile put them at ease.

"I know you have many questions, and I will attempt to answer each one as we embark on a journey that will change your lives," the pilot stated. "First, you are in a craft fondly named after an eagle. It was developed by a Mr. Darious Miller with funding from the Browning Foundation. The Browning Foundation was formed by Alonzo Browning and funded by his son, David. Through a series of events, that can only be credited to God, Darious and David came together to produce these crafts.

"They run on the abundant energy that God surrounded his creation with at the beginning of time. Man is just now learning to harness it. The technology to use this energy had been suppressed by ignorance and greed until now.

"You are here because God chose you. He did so because sometime in your walk, you chose Him! Only those with the Holy Spirit within are chosen. Whatever God has in store for you is between you and Him. Some of you will remain with us until the Second Coming. Some of you will be called to return to the world.

"The paper you touched is the uniting force and the reason you are here. You all saw a beautiful mural of our Lord Jesus Christ. Anyone not truly of the faith would see only random shapes and colors."

The monitor beeped for her attention. She swiveled around to face it and announced their imminent arrival.

"Where are we?" Marcus asked.

"You are going to one of a networks of settlements that will provide a haven. There is plenty of food, water, and fellowship. You will be safe there. You are free to leave whenever God puts on your heart to do so. Most will stay, but a few will be called to fight."

He meant physical location, but as the craft descend as the pilot tended to her duties, he did not want to distract her. The craft gently touched the landing pad, and the stairs lowered. They descended the ramp into a lush, green garden. It seemed every space that wasn't walkway was filled with fruit trees, or vegetables, or flowers. The fragrance had an immediate calming effect on all of the passengers. A young boy greeted them.

"Welcome! My name is James. If you follow me, I'll show you to your homes."

He seemed pleased that he had such an important part in their arrival. They followed him down a walkway leading into the base of a mountain. Inside were thousands of numbered doors bathed in a soft soothing light. Each person was assigned a number.

Marcus opened his door into a spacious room containing everything he needed, even a change of perfectly fitting clothes. The light seemed to emit from the walls and ceiling. The source was hard to determine, but it bathed him in soothing comfort.

A knock on his door startled him back to reality. He opened the door to a young man who extended his hand and introduced himself as Elias Tobias Montigue. Marcus grabbed the man's hand and returned the introduction.

"I'm Marcus Rashida. This is quite a place. How did you come to be here?"

"It's a long and interesting story, Mr. Rashida. We moved here from Detroit, Michigan, to develop and manufacture the craft that brought you here. The short version is that God has provided for our every need since we arrived. This is only one of many such places like this in the world. Why were you brought to this one? I don't know, but God will reveal the reason in his time."

Elias smiled and allowed his guest to soak in the information. "If you would, Marcus, walk with me in the garden, and I will answer any questions I can."

They walked in silence for a while until Marcus spoke. "I have with me two videos of what our world is plunging into. My best friend in college was the earthly step-father of the one they call the Beast. He recorded the Beast in the act of torturing and killing seven men for no other reason than to enjoy their pain and misery. I have another video of the Beast killing my friend, Yussaf. When he confronted his step-son, he was brutally murdered. The Beast must be stopped."

"Show this to our team and let us help you."

"I would be glad to, Elias."

"Tomorrow, after your sleep cycle? I'll send my son, James, to show you to breakfast."

"Yes, yes, I'll be there."

Elias walked him back to his quarters and left. Marcus was totally exhausted. He hadn't slept well since Yussaf's death. He tumbled onto his bed and fell into a deep and dreamless sleep.

A knock on his door woke him up. He hadn't stirred since he lay down. When he opened the door, it was the young boy, James, who greeted him on his arrival.

"Good morning!" he said cheerily. "We have breakfast prepared in the dining area. If you like, I can take you there."

"Come in, James. I need to wash up. I apologize for oversleeping."

"We have no day or night here because we operate on God's time. My dad says not to rush anyone. He told me about different time zones, and that the people who come here have been through a lot. I can come back if you want."

Marcus smiled at the boy. It was refreshing to find a child with such exuberance, and with a servant's heart.

"I'll be ready in a minute." Marcus grabbed the clothes provided for him and headed for the bathroom to change.

James sat on the edge of a chair, fidgeting with a globe on the stand next to the chair, almost bouncing with pent-up energy. When Marcus reentered the room, he jumped up and opened the door for Marcus, struggling with its weight, beaming when he succeeded.

"Lead the way, young man," Marcus said. Just being around the boy raised his spirit.

They walked down a lush garden walkway leading to the dining hall. Marcus could have easily plucked some fruit off one of the trees and eaten it for breakfast on the way.

The long table was lined with chairs. All arrivals from yesterday were present. They stood, linked together hand in hand, while Elias said a prayer. They all seated themselves, trying to get acquainted with one another, wondering what brought them together in this place.

Generous portions of Ful, a favorite Egyptian breakfast dish, were brought out by cheerful servers along with a variety of fruits and strong teas. Marcus savored the meal. It had been a long time since he had an appetite for anything. He enjoyed the conversation bantering around the table, each person trying to find common threads linking them together, and to this place.

"How are you this morning, Mr. Rashida?" Elias asked after everyone was finished.

"I'm better than I have been in a long while. Thank you."

"I've taken the liberty of inviting our team leaders and all of the staff to our briefing this morning. There is a reason that God brought you all together half-way around the world to a mountain in America, when we have compounds all over the world, many much closer to where you live."

"Good, the more people that can see what is coming to this world, the better," Marcus replied.

"My oldest son, Duane, will accompany you when you have finished enjoying your tea. I must attend to some details beforehand, but I'll see you soon."

Elias left the room. Marcus relaxed for the few minutes before his meeting, marveling at the circumstances that led him to this place. A boy approached Marcus. He bore a family resemblance to James. He looked a little older, but his mannerisms and facial features linked the two although he had a much calmer disposition.

"Mr. Rashida, my name is Duane. I am James' older brother. I was told to escort you to the meeting room. Please follow me."

Marcus followed, amused by his serious manner. He was all business, not as exuberant as his sibling, but the servants heart linked the two. They entered a large room with a conference table at the center lined with chairs. The people invited were already seated, talking among themselves.

A large black man at the head of the table rose and came toward Marcus.

"My name is Darious Miller, Mr. Rashida. I'm the CEO of Dubai International and current chairman of the board of the governing body of this Eden. Welcome to our facility and our family!"

He took Marcus' hand and shook it vigorously.

"Elias has briefed me on your presentation. I'm sorry for your loss. We will do everything God has planned to help you. The monitor control is here," he said, pointing to a small rectangular area just under the large conference table where Darious motioned Marcus to sit.

"Can I have your attention please? We are about to start this meeting. Let's Pray. After the opening prayer, Mr. Marcus Rashida will address us about the events he witnessed in Cairo."

The room fell silent while Darious prayed. Marcus rose and greeted everyone.

"I must warn you in advance the video you're about to see is graphic and uncensored. I want to bring to light the evil I witnessed from this man called the Beast by his unsuspecting, adoring fans. To them, he can do no wrong. Feel free to leave if the images become too intense."

The video ended to stunned silence.

He stood again and explained about the relationship of his friend, Yussaf, to the Beast and the reasons why they conspired to record the second video.

He sat down as the second video started and bowed his head and closed his eyes, steeling himself against the content. He knew it was necessary to share it, but it was extremely hard for him to witness again."

He could tell by the narrative and the gasps by the people in the room what part of the video was showing. Silence settled in the room like a cloud. He opened his eyes and rose to his feet.

"The presentation speaks for itself," he began. "I can't begin to tell you how painful it was to witness this again, but I felt I had to show it to get the word out about this monster. Most perceive him as the world's greatest soccer player, but this is only a stepping-stone to his true ambition, world domination. I am too close to this to be objective. I cannot help but feel he is unstoppable. I hope that someone in this room can show me how to take down the Beast."

He sat back down to silence. No one had yet recovered enough to offer anything but condolences to him for the loss of his friend.

Darious stood up and started to pray. Everyone in the room stood up with him and joined hands. When the session ended, he dismissed everyone in the room; shaking their hand or hugging them. They were all witness to the evil taking over the world. It united them in purpose. They filed out of the room in stunned silence.

11

God's Plan

E lias couldn't sleep with the images from the meeting rolling in his mind. He slipped out of his room and walked quietly into the garden. There were no distractions there. He felt closest to God when in the garden. He left the troubled images at the foot of the cross and asked God to help him understand what was going on.

He had been faithful since his conversion. Some of the things he had done on faith still puzzled him. The bit-chain technology he developed that allowed the silicon paper responsible for Marcus's arrival still puzzled him. Why would God who created the Universe need him to create a piece of technology to link humans? But then, why would He use Moses to bring His people to the Promised Land when He could have done it with a thought? Elias' genius analytical mind sometimes reeled when confronted with his Creator's plans.

Elias sat down and prayed. He emptied his mind to allow the Holy Spirit to work. As he bowed his head, a single thought overwhelmed him. It sent shivers down his spine. Of course, he thought. Satan can manipulate anyone born of the flesh, even Christians, by casting doubts, causing strife, and altering the outcome of their actions, but he is oblivious to the signals the camera emitted as the evil deeds were recorded.

God had just revealed the reason Elias had been commissioned to build the bit-chain technology linked to the silicon paper and the way he could help Marcus.

Elias hurried to his office and started working on his plan. It wasn't the end of his sleep cycle yet, and he had hours before anyone would start their day. He did his best work in solitude.

He walked into the breakfast gathering famished and exited, just in time to pray for the meal. When everyone sat down, he started telling them of his revelation. When they were finished, he asked them to attend a meeting in the conference hall where he could go into details about his idea.

The assembly sat in silence as Elias unfurled his revelation. "As I was walking last night in the garden, God brought me to a revelation. The reason we developed the bit-chain and the silicon paper to bring persecuted Christians to us is the same reason Marcus was brought to us.

"What is the common thread linking the two observations?" he asked, and then went on to answer his own query. "The link is the waves used to transmit the data in the bit-chain. In other words, the waves the camera used to transmit the data to the recording device are undetected by Satan and the Beast.

They all agreed. Elias was elated. He was happiest when he had a mission.

"The way to fight against the Beast is to use technology! I propose we create a specialized android whose function is to get us into the Beast's rallies and report the data to us. The android will have to be completely self-sufficient and programmable. These android machines already exist but would have to be modified, and reprogrammed. We have a few that we use in our manufacturing processes when the job is too toxic or dangerous for humans. They are crude in appearance and movement, but we could fix that and send them anywhere the Beast is, undetected."

"I would like to volunteer for this project, Elias," Marcus piped in. "I don't know much about the technology, but I know the Beast's movements and his cultural environment. I would be very helpful in showing the creators of the android how to make him authentic."

12

From the Beginning

C hione was not alone. Since the beginning of humans' reign on earth, there were Satan's servants. The chosen were human in form, flesh and blood, void of any spiritual capacity. They no longer possessed a soul, as they gave it to the darkness in exchange for immortality when Satan would become king of the world.

The culmination of her work, the ultimate summit of the ten most powerful leaders on Earth, was scheduled for January 6, the Beast's Day of birth. The newly elected presidents and prime ministers finally agreed that they could no longer ignore the Beast.

Her personal story started five-hundred years ago in a serf's cabin. She was born beautiful and charming, so she learned to use her wiles to gain access to the court of the local nobleman. Through treachery and deceit, she managed to become his wife for a short time until his "untimely" death. She moved on the king's court, where, through more treachery, deceit, and murder, she became queen.

The day before she was to be beheaded for infidelity and murder, the dark lord took notice of her talents and offered her eternal youth and immortality in exchange for her soul. A fair trade, she thought. Now it was her job to ensure her dark master was victorious in the oncoming plot for domination of the souls of Earth.

Only the vilest and most treacherous needed to apply to be her peers. Those were demons placed in high places in world politics, privy to the inner workings of every society on earth, the devil's advocate. Not the cartoon red devil perched on someone's shoulder, but the "person" across from the living, looking them in the eye, talking bent truths until the truth became a lie and the lie became the truth, perverting morals for the sake of power and control.

Satan had been amassing his army of legions since the beginning of time. Chione was a newcomer. It started when the serpent slithered out of the Garden of Eden with Adam and Eve, causing one son to kill the other. In the time of Noah, the only holy one left on earth, their success in perverting God's children resulted in the whole world being wiped out in a flood, except for one boat protected by

God. The possessed had been around since people started sinning against God. They had one thing in common—they sold their souls for the promise of earthly immortality when Satan reigned.

They weren't kings, but they were always in his court, planting ideas, fermenting greed, lust, and intrigue. The legions were always the ladle stirring the boiling cauldron, adding the arsenic to the stew, poisoning the minds of men and women, causing misery for the masses. The legions were in the camp of Israel, causing the whole nation to stray away from God and worship idols even as Moses was on the mountain with God.

They were on both sides of every war keeping the hatred glowing red as the blood on the battlefield. They did the bidding of their dark master with glee, and humankind was all too willing. Like sheep led to slaughter. They were about to come together in unprecedented numbers under a leader they had anticipated for centuries.

She knew the time was at hand. The prince of darkness walked the earth. All the preparations were finished. When he rose to power, the centuries of preparation would culminate in a reign without opposition. Her master's dark kingdom would extend from the world of lost souls to the entire surface of the earth. There would be no borders, only Earth and hell. She said a prayer to her dark master. She had many things to do. The Beast would address heads of state, and all the powerful in the world. If she pulled the correct strings, the world would be his.

The one troubling problem was the Beast's insatiable need to kill. His craving was getting out of hand. He required more and more victims. She already had a crew in the field continuously fishing for the right circumstances and criteria.

She was disturbed by the effect it was having on his appearance. Makeup and camera angles hid it from his public, but his face was aging. His hands were becoming bent and craggily, his skin becoming scaly and red. His twenty-seven-year-old features looked more like a man in his late forties.

Chione had never seen the face of Satan; he was always hidden by the mist. What if the darkness she embraced, the suffering and misery Satan promoted made him detestable to look at, the very reason for the darkness? The Beast couldn't be allowed that fate, at least not until he fulfilled his destiny. She had too much invested in him to fail now.

The next few months were a whirlwind of political rallies and closed-door power meetings. The Beast would no longer be just a soccer player. The next season would start without him. He was running for the Egyptian parliament.

He used his worldwide fame as a steppingstone. The Beast's charisma translated into a solid base of support for the position. His soccer skills paled in comparison to his political skill. His short stint as a member of the Egyptian parliament was a stepping-stone to greater things.

Never in her history had she heard anyone charm a crowd the way he did. She had been with Mao Zedong when he murdered his seventy-five million people, Joseph Stalin when he murdered his sixty-two million people, and at Hitler's side during the Third Reich when he exterminated so many Jews. But all of them together could not begin to match the Beast's charisma. From South Africa to Egypt, the nations of continental Africa embraced his political ambitions. More and more, the splintered factions, the rebel Islamic militants, the Marxist, the communists, and even some "Christian" militia pledged allegiance to him. All their ideologies were eradicated until there was only his ideology, only his thoughts. They had no choice after they witnessed his brutality firsthand. He was a power not to be opposed.

13

Methodical Madness

Many legions stood as he entered the room. The Beast had in his mind that he would be meeting with three (trilateral) legions instead of the banquet hall filled with men and women; hosts of thousands of legions.

"We've been waiting on you a long time, Master," said a withered-looking gentleman as he rose from his seat and bowed before the Beast. "Please be seated so we can answer any questions you may have about us."

The Beast acknowledged the group and sat down. No introductions were given.

"You are called the Trilateral Commission, but there are many more of you than three?" The Beast questioned.

"There have been rumors of a "Trilateral Commission" for centuries, the old man began. "The masses think there are three powerful families controlling the governments of the entire world. We let the rumors fly, and sometimes fuel the lies to help keep our true identify hidden. If anyone gets close to the truth, they meet an untimely death.

"We are the Trilateral because we control the three most important things on Earth: health, wealth, and water. They are intertwined. Humankind cannot exist without them. The legions in this room control all pharmaceutical manufacturers around the world. The bit-coin revolution has enabled us to control and monitor the movement of all wealth created and stored. We own every water-bottling company in the world."

"Get to the point," the Beast warned, agitated by the long narrative.

"Yes, Master. We have developed an odorless drug that can be added to the billions of water bottles distributed and consumed globally every day. This colorless, odorless compound is the most addictive substance on Earth and the one who controls distribution of it controls ninety-three percent of the population. According to our clinical trials, there are side effects. Up to three percent will die from reactions to the drug, and somewhere around five percent won't be affected."

A slow, evil smile crossed the Beast's face. "Is this ready for mass distribution?"

"Yes, Master," the legion replied.

"Good! I know just the place to begin the conquest! On January 6, my Birthday, I'll have a summit to negotiate with the ten most powerful leaders on the planet. We can start at the top and let it trickle down!"

He laughed an evil laugh at the joke. He left the meeting elated. He felt the need to feed his own addiction.

Chione was left in charge of the distribution of amygdaloideum, Amy for short. The most powerful weapon ever released on the face of the Earth. Less than a drop per five-hundred milliliter bottle gave control of a soul to the Beast. Tanker trucks rolled into every water-bottling plant in the world. The stage was set.

14

The Beginning of the End

Protocols were hashed out. The venue combed by security until every country was satisfied its leaders would be safe attending the summit. Negotiations, down to the seating arrangements, went on for weeks—so many egos to rub, delusions of grandeur to pacify. Chione worked tirelessly to appease every country. The paparazzi were instructed where to position to get the best side of these prima donnas. The reporters were handpicked to deliver the best narrative to the countries back home.

The Beast had a long way to go to bring the fragmented world into compliance, but he felt the power of fulfilling his destiny.

The Beast did his homework. The countries' dignitaries' arrival times were spaced two hours apart so he could greet each one individually. He turned on his charm and used his extensive research about each individual to become like family. He spoke to each flawlessly in their own language as if they were old friends.

It was time. Chione introduced Each dignitary as they entered.

"The honorable Sheik Mansouri, representing the great nation of the United Arab Emirates.

"The royal King Saud Al-Faisal, representing the great nation of Saudi Arabia.

"The honorable Nakamura Kysoshi, representing the great nation of Japan.

"The honorable Friedman Goldwasser, representing the great nation of Israel.

"The honorable Claude Blanchete, representing the great nation of France.

"The honorable Wilhelm Konig, representing the great nation of Germany.

"The honorable Jonathan Gabriel, representing the great nation of the United Kingdom.

"The honorable Wang Wai, representing the great nation of China.

"The honorable Oreal Stepanov, representing the great nation of Russia.

"The honorable Michele Stalwart, representing the great nation of the United States."

The Beast escorted each one personally to their seats, chatting as if they were old friends. When the procession ended, he walked to his seat and raised the clear goblet of water in front of him.

"One of the first things we need to address in this summit is how to provide clean, clear water to each and every person on the planet. As you know, the population explosion, pollution, and climate change threaten the supply of drinkable water. I propose a toast, to clean water for everyone."

They nodded unanimously and clinked glasses around the table. *This is the only time they will ever agree on anything!* he thought, beaming, holding his glass high. The experiment began. He observed each one as they took their turn speaking, voicing their country's concerns and expectations for the summit.

By this time tomorrow the effects of amygdaloideum would start. If the ones who ingested it didn't get their daily dose within hours of the last dose, paranoia would take over. The Beast watched each one closely as they gave their introductory speeches. He observed that each and every one discretely sipped the water provided in the goblets until it was gone.

The following day, the Beast greeted the world leaders as they filed into the room at the appointed time. They seemed subdued, as if they were hung over from a night of drinking. The summit resumed.

Chione was the acting chairperson of the meeting.

She called the meeting to order. That was the last thing the group agreed on. Each country's representative vied for control of the podium, not following protocol.

The verbal melee came to an end when Chione recognized Wang Wai of China.

"Before we can solve any problems like clean water for the planet, we must establish our governing protocol; who will host the headquarters of the New World Order? As the most populous nation on earth, I make a motion to establish it in the city of Beijing.

He was interrupted by everyone. Chione struggled to maintain control.

"The chair recognizes Oreal Stepanov of Russia."

"Just how are we going to establish the leadership of this governing body?"

He had been secretly lobbying, bribing, and coercing the other countries; establishing his political power base.

Chaos erupted again. As the morning wore on, the group seemed to get more short- tempered. Their testy exchanges resembled a fight between rival gangs more than the savviest politicians in the world. The Beast rose from his chair and took Chione's gavel and pounded on the table until order was restored.

"I propose another toast. May calmer heads prevail!" He raised his glass as did the others. As he looked around the room, the participants chugged the cup like drunkards anticipating the calming high of the first drink of the night.

"Let us adjourn for lunch and come back refreshed and ready to tackle the problems at hand," he said.

They all filed out bickering and posturing like roosters. Security actually came between some to prevent physical violence.   The Beast smiled. Two hours later, they filed in talking and laughing, ready to meet the challenges head on.

The Beast scheduled his speech for the end of the day. He rose slowly to the podium. The silence in the room spoke volumes of the respect he commanded. He paused a moment before his booming voice filled every corner of the room.

"Esteemed leaders, I would like to propose a new world. One void of the borders we so diligently protect. One void of the religious strife we all experience every day; one where hunger and thirst for clean water do not exist. Don't we belong to the same species? We all bleed red if we're cut. We all share the same chromosomes of life! Why, besides pride and power, should we spend so much of the precious resources of this planet on weapons of war when we could be solving the pressing problems of our time?"

"Here are my proposals, short and to the point."

1.   We elect a council to oversee the transition to one leader. This council will answer to the Beast, the supreme leader. All countries would keep their

governing bodies, to tend to day-to-day problems unique to their region.

2.   All militaries surrender to the Beast. All nuclear weapons will be destroyed on a rotating basis until every weapon is gone. Open verification will be conducted by the military.

3.   All religions will be banned. In this progressive age, they are no longer relevant. We can spend that energy on repairing the damage inflicted on humanity in the name of a worthless deity.

4.   All cultures will be assimilated in time into one by interaction and intermarriage.

5.   The New World Order will control all wealth and divide it equally so all poverty can be eliminated.

When he sat down, the whole room erupted, arguing among themselves about his proposals, all fearful of losing power, prestige, and wealth. No one considering the people they were supposed to be representing.

Stalin, Mao, Hitler, every dictator that walked the planet had these same ideas. The Beast wasn't original in his doctrine. They all shook their condescending heads in denial as they filed out of the room.

The third and final day started like the second day. All the leaders of the most powerful nations on

Earth bickered and fought like siblings. They finally sat down as the Beast called the summit to order. In the silence he began to speak.

"You will find on your desk my proposal from yesterday. I suggest you look it over and sign it making me the president of the New World Order, turning over your authority to me. If you do, you will be retained as liaisons with your country and become leaders of a new world order like this planet has never seen.

The one that seemed to be the most agitated, Claude Blanchete of France, got up and shook his fist at the Beast, cursing in French.

"If you think I'm going to betray my country like that, you're insane!"

The Beast got up from his chair and calmly said to the Frenchman, "Sir, you need to calm down and think this through."

When the Frenchman continued his tirade, the Beast walked over to his position slowly, as if trying to calm him down. Quicker than the eye could perceive, the Frenchman was dangling in the air with the Beast's hand around his neck, his thumb crushing into the Frenchman's windpipe. With a whipping jerk, the man's skull was dislocated from his neck. The Beast couldn't help but drink in the terror of death before he threw the man down in a heap, convulsing and twitching as his soul left him. In the stunned silence, the Beast walked back to his chair.

"Please be seated!" he said in a lion-like voice. When they complied, he spoke, "I'm afraid Mr. Blanchete will miss the most important part of my presentation. With all the excitement just now, most of you are feeling terror and fear. I think that the Frenchman has made my presentation doubly hard. You see, the emotions you feel right now are not entirely because of the circumstances you witnessed.

"On the first day, when we toasted to clean, unpolluted water for all, you were given a substance called amygdaloideum, Amy for ease of pronunciation. It affects the amygdale in your brain that control emotions such as fear, rage, and terror. It is the most addictive substance on the planet.

"Notice the goblets in front of you contain no water. In less than two hours, you will be shivering imbeciles, curled in a fetal position, not good for anything. None of us want that, so sign the directive and we will give you your daily ration of Amy.

"Before you get any delusions of sacrificing yourself for the good of your country, know that, for weeks, we have been distributing this in the bottled water around the world thanks to my friends in the Trilateral Commission. So far, we have been supplying everyone with enough to keep them stable. Any disruption and we will cease distribution, leaving you with mindless anarchists for countrymen roaming the streets with the sole purpose of finding their next bottle of Amy."

He stopped talking so they could confer. They talked among themselves, getting more paranoid as the minutes ticked off. He waited patiently.

"Mr. Blanchete made a terrible miscalculation when he showed such impertinence. His country will suffer the consequences of not joining our movement voluntarily. Observe what happens to the cities in France when I cut off the supply of Amy. Within days, the proud and vibrant city of Paris will fall into chaos. It will be an example of my power. If you will not sign the accord, you can be my guests as we watch the carnage."

He brought out bottles of Amy for them to see. The bottles were guarded by a platoon of large, well-armed men. One by one, the dignitaries lost their dignity. Like puppies being trained to accept a treat for good behavior, they signed and got their reward.

The Beast knew that not every citizen of every country would be tainted by the water, but the numbers were in the billions that would, a readymade army, willing to do his bidding over any other authority on Earth. The trillions of bit-coin in his coffers would make sure they were well armed. The water would keep them loyal.

He marveled at the simplicity of his plan. With all the weapons of mass destruction, each country possessed they were helpless to resist. He said a prayer of thanks to his master.

One by one, they grabbed the bottle offered to them after signing the agreement. They chugged the water like people walking out of the dessert into an oasis. It wasn't thirst they were quenching, but an uncontrollable craving felt deep in the brain. Collectively they stood, using the table for support, breathing like a runner, heart pounding, anticipating the calm brought on by the drug.

"We signed that document under duress!" Friedman Wasserman of Israel exclaimed. "No court of any country will recognize it!"

The others nodded in agreement, still reeling from the withdrawal, even the Arab leaders, who normally wouldn't even shake the Jew's hand were united, but helpless and they knew it! The Beast had conquered the world without firing a shot!

The chaos in every land seemed to cross every ethnic, racial, or political barrier. The rich, the poor, every faction and splinter group of every nation took to the streets to search for relief from their suffering. Drug dealers ran out of drugs to sell. They were mauled by the raging zombies roaming the streets. Every hospital and pharmacy were stripped bare in the quest for relief.

The Beast broadcast a live feed to every nation on Earth with an edited version of the events at the summit in every language on the planet. It didn't show the death of the Frenchman; it wasn't yet time.

"Recent events have unfolded before you. The chaos and violence that threatens to undermine the very existence of civilization is caused by the most addictive substance known to exist, amygdaloideum. It has been infused into every bottle of water manufactured in the world. I have restricted the availability of the water to demonstrate the devastating effect it has on humanity. At the present time, there is no cure or antidote. I control the supply. With total compliance to my directives, the supply will go on uninterrupted."

"The directive has been sent to every governing body in the world. As soon as I get a signed directive bringing a region into compliance, I will resume delivery to that region. I will be waiting for a reply."

"In the name of the New World Order, by Satan's servant, Goodbye."

15

The Chosen

Marcus watched the broadcast in horror. He was ready to buy a bottle of water when he heard the news. He had been living between his modest apartment in Cairo and the Eden he was sent to, delivering the silicon papers to the people and collecting data on the movements of the Beast and his posse. The priority now was not stopping the Beast but providing a safe haven for the mass of Christians soon to be hunted like animals. He could still move freely in the streets of the city checking his contacts and holding small worship services. It was time for him to report to Elias.

Marcus still marveled at the network that existed throughout the world for the faithful. He needed the renewal and companionship of his fellow Christians on his weekly trips.

I'm so glad I never married, he thought. His true love was his Christ and the God he served. He was free to move to and from each world without worry of jeopardizing a family.

Elias would be interested in the latest development. The network Elias and his faithful followers built on faith would soon be sorely tested. Marcus touched the paper and saw the location for the latest rendezvous.

His anxiety eased when the ramp lowered and he found himself once again in the protection of his Lord. He learned to appreciate the time he spent in the Eagle traveling, meditating. He felt the familiar heaviness as the craft accelerated. As soon as he landed, he sought out Elias.

"Elias, my good friend!" Marcus said while greeting him with his Eastern traditional kiss on each cheek along with the Western hand shake. He sensed Elias was uncomfortable with it at first but embraced it as their friendship grew. "I have some very disturbing news, Elias. The Beast has made his move."

"We have heard the rumors, but I need to hear it from you my friend," replied Elias.

"The biggest news is don't drink the water! A new compound has been developed, and when ingested, it addicts most people instantly. The Beast and his Trilateral Commission control the supply, and there is no known antidote or substitute. My research shows that about eighty percent of the population is affected, depending on what region of the world we're talking about."

Elias was deep in thought, trying to calculate the number of people in his head. He snapped back to reality. "I almost forgot, there is someone I'd like for you to meet."

They walked down a corridor that opened into a large laboratory. A man sat with his back to them. At least, Marcus thought it was a man.

"Marcus, I'd like to introduce you to DAN, short for derived algorithmic neuroplasm. His name refers to the plasma that floods his artificial brain receptors. This plasma is affected by the slightest change in the electrons passing through it. The compounds "remember" by forming atomic structures linking atoms together in a unique chain that can be retrieved any time."

DAN swiveled around in his chair when he heard his name. He got up to greet the two guests.

"DAN, this is Marcus. Marcus, this is DAN."

"Pleased to meet you, Marcus," the machine said in a low, monotone voice.

"We have taken DAN as far as we can in the laboratory. He has a vocabulary as large as a college professor and the social skills of a savant. He has no experience in the real world where nothing is as it seems. We will have to rely on you to teach him how to react in real world situations."

Marcus began by sticking his right hand out in a handshake while looking the machine in the eye to see its response. The eyes were lifelike, but were devoid of any emotion. The machine responded to his handshake gesture.

"The more you interact with DAN, the more he will learn. He will pick up on your emotional response and adopt it as his own. You are his father, his mother, and his mentor. With the proper stimulus, he will learn in seconds what a human child would in its entire school experience.

"He is powered by the same energy that allows the Eagles to operate. He requires no outside power source, but he needs to shut down periodically to analyze his input and categorize the information into useful data. Currently, his pupils are equipped with powerful cameras that can see much clearer than a human. We have installed sensors under the surface of his palms so he can download his data when he returns to us. We don't want to transmit any signal in case the security people around the Beast are monitoring. When you return to the world, he will go with you."

Marcus pondered over what Elias said as he studied DAN. They would attend the frequent rallies that the Beast hosted to learn all they could about his movements, weaknesses, and strengths.

Know your enemy! thought Marcus.

DAN became Marcus' constant companion from that time on.

"Elias, we need to talk about the situation outside. Many of the unsuspecting population that ingested Amy were likely Christians. I can't believe our God would allow a Holy Spirit-filled convert to be lost this way. God has put it on my heart to make sure these people have a chance to kick this dependence on the devil. I propose we bring in those that have the fingerprint of faith and surround them with prayer. This place heals. It has done wonders for me! If they are true children of God, He will surely heal them."

"I agree, Marcus. I need to confer with the governing board so we can have a plan in place for their arrival."

"In the meantime, why don't you recharge and renew? We may get precious little time to do that in the coming deluge," Elias suggested.

Marcus made his way to his room with DAN walking beside him, step for step. DAN sat in the chair motionless. Marcus enjoyed another peaceful night of rest bathed in the soft light. He wished he didn't have to leave this place, but there were so many in need now that he couldn't ignore the call. They would leave after the next sleep cycle. He would have to take note of the date when he got back to Cairo. Since there was no day or night in Edens, only the healing light, he lost track of the worldly time.

He woke rested and ready to re-enter the world. They were given their allotment of the silicon papers to give to whomever God chose. Marcus tried to understand how the small number they were given could possibly do any good with such a need, but they never ran out. He thought of the seven loaves and seven fishes Jesus used to feed the five-thousand. The subtle miracles he had witnessed since he found this place gave him hope in a hopeless situation. Thousands just like him roamed the world giving the faithful an escape from the madness.

They boarded the craft for the flight. A short time later, they walked down the ramp to a small group of people waiting.

He smiled and reassured them, "You're going home!"

"What day is this, friend?" he asked the nearest one.

"It is March 6," the man answered.

It was exactly two months since the first dose of Amy hit the unsuspecting masses.

Marcus and DAN walked out of the secluded spot into the morning sun. Marcus heard a convoy of large trucks rolling down the street in the distance. Marcus was totally unprepared for what they encountered when they walked out of the side street into the main thoroughfare. As far as they could see were makeshift tents. A large sign above the street read "Distribution Center."

The stench of human feces and urine slapped Marcus in the face. DAN was unaffected, but Marcus' gag reflex caused him to retch. The flies buzzed in a low-pitched frenzy as they feasted.

The trucks Marcus heard in the background rolled to a stop in front of the sign, causing a mob. The mass of humanity, if they could still be classified as such, growled and jostled for position. One man, visibly trembling, with a rabid animal look in his eyes climbed over the crowd to the top of the truck.

A large well-armed guard shot him point-blank in the chest. The force of the point-blank laser round blew him off the truck into the street. He bled out instantly. The flies' symphony changed pitch as they swarmed around the still warm corpse. No one noticed or cared.

Their focus was on the bottles being distributed to anyone who had enough in their bit-card account to pay. After two months of the extortion, many were already penniless and homeless. The ones who couldn't pay were forcibly thrown out of the line. They begged and pleaded for just a taste from the lucky ones who scored, but their pleas were ignored.

Most opened the containers on the spot and downed the liquid immediately, discarding the bottles on the sidewalk.

The Jackal, as he was referred to, swooped in and fought over the empty bottles, barely letting them hit the ground. He wore a trench coat type outer garment with pockets lining the inside. When he had as many empty bottles as he could handle, he disappeared into his makeshift tent.

Marcus watched him through the partially closed tent flap. The Jackal carefully placed every bottle upright so none of the contents would spill. One by one, he placed them upside down on a funnel dripping into a glass container. When he was satisfied the plastic bottle wouldn't yield any more liquid, he removed it and placed another one on the funnel. He reached under his bed matt and took out a knife and filleted the bottle, exposing the inside. He licked every bit of the inside so none of the precious liquid would escape. He repeated the routine until every bottle was processed. He fell back on his matt exhausted. He hadn't eaten for days, but that didn't matter so long as he got enough of Amy to stave off the madness.

Marcus noticed one man take his ration and stash it in a stainless-steel container strapped securely to his chest. When he moved his shirt to deposit the bottle, Marcus saw a large military style knife stuck in his belt. As soon as the man secured the bottle, he left in a hurry. Marcus and DAN ran after him. They saw him enter a large apartment building.

The man didn't have the look of the addicts on the street. He was a muscular, well-dressed man, and he was in a hurry to get as far away from the chaos outside as possible. Marcus and DAN caught up with him waiting on the elevator.

"Sir, could I talk to you for a minute?" asked Marcus, walking toward the man.

"Keep your distance!"

His knife pointed at Marcus' chest instantly.

Marcus stepped back, but quicker that the eye, DAN grabbed the wrist of the man with one hand and peeled the knife out of his clenched fist with the other.

"Don't take it, it's for my wife!" he said, referring to the precious bottle.

"We don't want your water, but we'd like to ask you some questions. We weren't here when this started and want to understand what's going on."

DAN handed him back his knife.

Marcus reached in his folder and handed a paper to the man. As soon as the man touched the silicon paper, all the anxiety left him. Tears streamed down his face. Hope. For the first time since Amy was unleashed, he felt hope for the future.

"What is this?" he asked.

"Tell me, what do you see?"

"I see a picture of Jesus on the cross."

"Then this is your ticket to Eden, a place created by the works of God for all believers in these end times. Anyone who sees this image will be taken to a place of renewal and joy like you have never experienced."

"How does this work? I want to know more details before I can believe anything a stranger claims! The truth is scarce in these times." Asked the man.

"I must admit, I don't know all the details or the technology, but Just as God supplied all the manna the Israelites needed on their trek to the promised land, He has provided all that we need in these hard times. You just need to have faith that he will take care of you."

The man contemplated what Marcus said for a minute. Hope was scarce in these desperate times.

He wanted to believe Marcus but doubted his offer.

He finally shook his head, "I cannot go."

Marcus looked at him puzzled. "Why not? He's offering you safe haven."

"When I drank the tainted water, I fell very sick with convulsions and fever, but after a few days, I recovered and couldn't stand the thought of ever drinking it again. Some of my friends died from the effects. My wife who is seven months' pregnant needs it every day to function. I get it to her every day before I go to work. It takes half of my daily income now to purchase this one bottle. The soldiers raise the price weekly. Soon no one will be able to buy it. We will have to move. I can't afford food and rent. I fear we may end up in the strect like so many have already."

"Is your wife also a believer?"

"Yes"

"Then let us go to her."

The elevator door opened and they stepped inside. The man pressed the   fourth-floor button. They rode in silence but the man prayed softly that this new hope would extend to his wife. He would not abandon her and their child for his own safety. The door opened and they walked down a hall to apartment four twenty-nine. The door opened to a sparsely furnished but well-kept apartment. On the sofa, lying in a fetal position was a woman covered in a heavy blanket, shivering like she was on a bed of ice.

"Did you get it?" she asked.

He removed the bottle from its protective sheath, removed the cap, and handed it to her.

She drank it all without hesitation. She sat on the couch gently rocking in anticipation of the magic healing the water possessed, barely aware of the presence of two strangers with her husband. Awkward silence froze time while the healing worked. Marcus noticed her emaciated frame and hollow eyes. She obviously wasn't eating properly. Side effects of the drug, he thought.

She took notice of her surroundings, rising to her feet, shedding the blanket like a cocoon. Embarrassed, she gave her husband a look that would melt iron.

"Why would you bring total strangers to witness me in my weakest, most vulnerable moment?"

He caught the hurt in her stare and stammered awkwardly to save the moment by introducing his new friends,

"I...I don't know your names!" he said, panicked, caught in his oversight, looking at Marcus and DAN.

Marcus attempted to rescue his newest acquaintance, "My name is Marcus Rashida, and this is my android body guard DAN."

"This is my wife, Sabella, and I am Steven. I mean, we are Sabella and Steven Bishara."

Marcus smiled and greeted Steven with the proper greeting.

"I feel like old friends, Steven."

Marcus nodded toward Sabella and pointed toward the paper in Steven's hand. The paper magnified the trembling of his hand as he passed the paper to Sabella.

"Take this paper and tell me what you see," Steven stated with the same anticipation he felt when he asked her to marry him.

Her face glowed. The baby in her womb moved and kicked so that she had to sit down. The joy welled up in her like the light feeling of topping a hill at speed.

"I see the Christ on the cross!"

Steven took her in his arms and danced around the room lightly, mindful of the precious life she was carrying.

"What do we do now?" he asked Marcus.

"Be still and listen to your inner self. A craft will appear to gather you for a journey to the safe haven. Take nothing from this world. Everything you need will be provided."

"I need to know more before I commit my family to this. How did this come about? What is the reason and the motive?"

"I will tell you what little I know. A young man by the name of Elias Tobias Montague heads the Eden that I am assigned to. He is a computer genius that developed software that enables the incredible machines you will be gathered in for your journey to operate. He is instrumental in..."

Steven interrupted Marcus. "I develop computer software! Elias is a legend in our circle. We were told that he died in a high-rise apartment building in Dubai. Elias is an alias for David Browning, the computer whiz kid that turned the bit-coin world upside down and became a multi-billionaire over night at the age of 16!"

"I assure you; he is alive and well and living in the first Eden to be developed." Replied Marcus.

Steven was convinced.

Steven and Sabella looked at each other and embraced. She knew by the look on her husband's face that this was genuine. This was the first time since Amy that they had any hope of escape from this hopeless, stifling existence.

"Will I get to meet Elias?" Asked Steven.

"I don't know, there are many Edens and it is up to God which one you are sent to."

Marcus took them by the hand and prayed for their safety. He knew he would never see this young couple again. He prayed silently that the treatment for her addiction would work. It was now entirely up to God.

Steven and Sabella looked around the modest apartment they had called home since they were married. Sabella had tears in her eyes as they headed for the door into an uncertain future.

Steven stopped abruptly and whispered something in Sabella's ear. She nodded.

"Could you use the apartment while you are in town?" he asked Marcus. "We have paid it up until the end of the month and would be honored if you could."

"That would solve one of our immediate problems! Yes, Steven we would be grateful. This will be a good place to stay while we gather our information on the Beast. Thank You."

Steven handed the keypad to Marcus and once again headed out the door with his bride. Once again, he stopped.

"It just occurred to me that the best way to keep an eye on the Beast is to attend his rallies. I have season tickets to the stadium. Sabella and I had to sell off the tickets to buy the Amy but the remaining season is still available. You can have those."

"See how God provides!" exclaimed Marcus, "We would be honored to accept your offer."

Steven and Sabella left quickly before they changed their minds.

16

The Great Physician

Steven and Sabella walked to a secluded part of a city park. It was getting dark and they were more than a little apprehensive about being out so late. Sabella clung to Steven. They came on a small clearing with a handful of people. They sensed that this was where they were being led.

A soft light appeared revealing a stairway. They entered the short stairs and found it led into some sort of aircraft. The pilot greeted them and requested they get comfortable and strap in to the available seats. He noticed the very pregnant woman and reprogrammed his ascent speed. He didn't want to deliver a baby on his last flight of the cycle!

When everyone was safely strapped in, he took off, talking, reassuring everyone constantly as the flight unfolded.

"The craft you are in is called an Eagle. It was made possible by a collaboration of the Browning foundation, Darious Miller, and a man known by two names, David Browning, or Elias Tobias Montague."

Steven's eyes opened wide and he nudged Sabella, trying to share his excitement.

"Excuse me sir, are we going to meet this man called David?" he asked the pilot.

"No, he is stationed at a different Eden on the other side of the world, but the people here are just as competent at handling your addiction. You see, there are people on this flight that are addicted to the Amy. We have been instructed to take you to the Eden most equipped to handle this problem. The people in charge here are all former Amy addicts and have been healed.

Steven and Sabella exchanged glances and held hands tightly, more convinced than ever they had made the right choice.

The pilot didn't quit talking until he gently set them down in the Eden. The only sensation of flying was the heaviness of the g-force at takeoff and a slight shudder as the craft descended. The pilots were at a loss to explain the slight turbulence when landing in the Eden. It didn't occur at any other time in landing, just in the Eden.

The floor lowered with a whoosh, turning into a stairway as it descended. The travelers exited into a new world. A soft light seemed to permeate everything. A sense of peace and joy bathed the new arrivals.

When they recovered enough to ponder what was next in their journey they were greeted by a middle-aged woman.

Mary Ellen was her name but everyone just called her mom. She exuded maternal love. She made it her personal responsibility to make everyone feel at home.

She introduced herself to the couple, soon to be three. She sensed the apprehension in them and decided to relate her own story.

"I was a doctor on the outside, until the government started telling me who I could treat and how I could treat them. When the Amy addiction hit, I poured all of my resources into a research facility to find a cure for the malady. My clinic was burned to the ground."

"I was jobless, soon to be homeless, and addicted to the vile Amy."

"I was raised in a Christian home but didn't feel the need to follow my parent's beliefs. God had provided the building blocks for scientific discovery and I followed the science. I didn't feel the need for any kind of personal relationship with God. Until the Amy destroyed my life."

"I sold my last piece of jewelry for a fraction of what it was worth to buy the last bottle of Amy I could afford. I couldn't go back home, my bank evicted me. I wondered the streets aimlessly, fretting about my last tomorrow. I was keenly aware of what happened to people that didn't get their daily fix of the Amy. Within forty-eight hours they tear their own flesh seeking relief from the madness until they bled to death."

"In my aimless wonderings I passed a church. The property looked abandoned and the door was unlocked so I entered the ransacked building. Everything of value was gone except the alter. I made my way to the front and fell on my knees at that alter. In my youth I saw many desperate people in hopeless positions just like me, kneel at the altar and come away comforted."

"My cries echoed in the empty church; please help me Lord! I know I have no right to ask but I can't survive on my own. I am tethered to a terrible master and I don't know how to fight it."

"Forgive me Lord for ignoring you all these years."

"I sobbed with my head buried in my hands. Tears wet the wooden bench where so many sinners had knelt before me."

"I surrender all Lord! I have very little to offer, I will be dead in forty-eight hours unless you intervene, I wailed."

"I rocked back and forth in my grief until I was exhausted. When I rose to leave, I noticed a piece of silicon paper on the alter. I was sure it wasn't there before. I looked around for the individual that could have put it there but the was no one."

"It had a kaleidoscope of colors in an abstract pattern. I was compelled to touch it. When I did a wave of relief settled over me. I saw the picture of My Savior on the cross and was reminded of all the childhood bible stories my mother told."

"I walked out of the church with a renewed inner strength. Somehow, I knew where I had to be. When I came to the clearing in the local park, I saw the stairway leading into some sort of craft. It was dark and its features were obscured."

"I was about to take my first step into the bird when I stopped cold. A voice inside me said, "that vile bottle cannot go with you.""

"I looked down at the bottle. I didn't realize I was clutching it like a child would a security blanket. I argued with the voice."

"But this bottle will give me one more day. I sold everything I have for it!"

"I am offering you eternity," said the voice."

"I knew my new found faith was being tested. I thought of the misery the bottle represented and tossed it into the darkness. Even if I do die tomorrow, I will be free of this addiction! I thought."

"I walked up the stairs with my head held high and my future uncertain."

"I remembered exiting the craft into a garden bathed in a soft light. Everything was so healthy and fresh. I still remembered when Mattie greeted me. Her name was Matilda but she preferred Mattie."

"Welcome to our Eden," she said."

"Thank you," I replied with a formal no-nonsense doctor's attitude. I wanted to warn Mattie and her staff of the impending monster within me."

"It is so calm and peaceful here. I hate to break it to you but I'm addicted to the Amy. In a few short hours I'll be a monster that will shatter that peace."

"Mattie only smiled and hugged me."

"You don't understand! I will slip into a madness you can do nothing about unless you have an antidote for Amy addiction."

"Mattie didn't seem to get the severity of what I was trying to convey. It infuriated me!"

"We don't have a cure for your addiction but God knows your plight. Just have faith." Mattie assured, "now let's get you settled."

"I remembered my apprehension at not being able to share my sense of urgency with Mattie."

"When Mattie showed me to my quarters I found a set of new clothes laid out on my new bed in just my size. I turned and saw my reflection in the vanity mirror.

At first, I didn't recognize that disheveled, dirty face staring back. Why would God even bother with me I thought."

"I held the clothes under my chin, imagining what I would look like wearing them. With new resolve I thought, If I'm living my last hours, I'm going to live them looking the best I can."

Mary Ellen could see that the new arrivals were spellbound by her story. She continued;

"I set about the task of removing the superficial evidence of my addiction. I showered and dressed and fixed my hair. I stared in the mirror and liked what I saw. I walked back into my new bedroom."

"There was Mattie waiting for me, "You look beautiful miss Mary Ellen!' she exclaimed."

"I blushed like a schoolgirl. I couldn't remember the last time someone had said that to me."

Sabella giggled at her comments, totally understanding.

"Thank You, I said."

"Mattie took me by the hand and led me to a dining area."

"Now we need to get you something to eat, she said."

"I remember how good that first meal tasted. My priority on the outside was to get the Amy; food was always secondary."

"My last meal I thought at the time."

"When I finished, Mattie escorted me back to my room."

"Sweet dreams she said at the door."

"I readied for bed. I was sure I wouldn't sleep a wink anticipating the withdrawal monster slowly taking my sanity."

"My slumber was disturbed by a knock on the door. I hurriedly dressed and answered."

"Mattie stood in the doorway."

"Are you ready to eat breakfast?" she asked."

""Breakfast? How long have I been asleep?" I inquired."

"Why, the whole sleep cycle. Don't ask me how long that is in minutes or hours because that time is irrelevant here. We only know sleep cycle and awareness cycle. Right now, you and I are in our awareness cycle."

"Why am I not in withdrawal, Mattie?" I asked."

"Mattie smiled a knowing smile and said to me, "Out there it was called the "practice" of medicine, right?"

"Yes, I replied."

"Here we are under the care of the Great Physician. He doesn't have to practice! chuckled Mattie."

"I experienced the same addiction as you and was healed right from the time I entered his care, she added."

Mary Ellen chuckled as she reminisced.

"Welcome to Eden," she exclaimed.

• • •

"Let me take you to your new place so you can settle in and freshen up for a meal. You both look like you could use some food," Mary Ellen said when she finished her story, "and by the way, Mattie was right! I'm here to testify!"

Mary Ellen never got tired of telling her story. She loved the reaction she got from all the new arrivals and especially these two young people. They were more at ease when she left them alone to get settled.

17

The Rally

I'*m glad Steven gave us these season tickets to the Beast's rallies at Borge El Arab Stadium* thought Marcus. *It will sure make it easier to infiltrate and learn about his movements and his habits.*

Marcus remembered what Steven said before he and Sabella left, "Yes. Since I have season ticket seats for the Pharaohs, I get priority at the stadium. I sell them now to make ends meet."

"Tomorrow night, he will be speaking at Borge El Arab Stadium where I have seats. I will give you the tickets, but you will be expected to buy a bottle of Amy. Be careful, people disappear for a single bottle! It is sold at the real price at the stadium, not the inflated prices that the soldiers demand. That way the Beast fills the stadiums."

"We are preparing to leave. Why don't you stay here while you are in town? I'll give you the code for the door. I've paid until the end of the month so someone might as well use it." Marcus remembered Steven saying.

Marcus and DAN spent the rest of the day distributing the silicone papers and gathering intelligence. It was nice to actually have a place to stay close to where they were assigned.

Marcus was considered a fugitive now. He didn't check in with the conforming behavior officer the last cycle, so he forfeited his apartment and possessions. He would be imprisoned for the rest of his life if caught, or used as fodder in the Beast's warped games.

The streets were calm as they made their way to the apartment for the night. The tents were still there, but the people subdued. The only thing that remained of the poor retch that stormed the truck was a splattering of reddish-brown stains on the pavement. Marcus shuddered, remembering his dream.

Apartment four twenty-nine was a welcome haven for the two. Marcus foraged for something to eat in the fridge. He found some goat cheese and made some tea. DAN sat motionless in a chair oblivious to the world around him while he processed his data.

Marcus crawled into bed exhausted, but sleep wouldn't come. All of the events of the day churned in his mind. He envied DAN. He wished he could make some sense of the madness gripping the world. DAN's brain would eventually shut down and rest, but his would not.

The morning sun's light broke through the window. The rays fell on still restless Marcus. He gave up on sleep and climbed out of bed, stumbling to the kitchen to see if he could brew some tea. He was thankful the Realm hadn't yet found a way to put the Amy in the tap water. DAN was still motionless in the chair. His external sensors alerted him of Marcus' movement and he followed Marcus around the room with his eyes.

Marcus found some bread and jam and sat down with his tea. Eyes closed, he bowed his head over the tea, felt the warmth, and smelled the strong aroma. *I hope my eyes are not as bloodshot as they feel,* he thought to himself. He munched on his bread, nibbled the cheese and sipped his tea, staring out the window as the water trucks pulled up and the mob gathered.

At least no one was shot today, he thought when they left, ashamed of his callous attitude. He tidied up, monitoring the events below. There was no use trying to go anywhere until the mob was appeased. He thought about this scene being repeated all over the world and shuddered. Humanity was chained to a cruel master.

When the trucks pulled away, Marcus and DAN headed out the door. They had papers to distribute and souls to save. They wandered through the city, but not aimlessly. There was always an unseen guide.

The Beast's rally would be the last stop of the day. Marcus didn't know what to expect from the rally. He had never been to that stadium. He was probably the only one from Cairo who never attended a football game.

The majestic old stadium stood bathed in the afternoon sun. At the sunset the shadow cast by the structure caressed the line of people entering.

Marcus was apprehensive as they swiped the tickets Seth had provided. The security arm swung open and they were in.

Some people ran to the booths as soon as they gained entry to buy Amy. Some drank it instantly while others stashed it. Marcus wondered if the stashed bottles were for loved ones or would find their way onto the black market. He bought his bottle and stashed it in his vest.

He and DAN made their way to the assigned seats. When he sat down and looked out on the arena, a strange feeling came over Marcus. He had been there before! But he knew he hadn't. The chill of realization made his whole body shiver. His dream, he was in the stadium of his dream!

Nausea welled from within and he desperately wanted to leave but the crowd was on their feet chanting "Beast! Beast! Beast!" There was no escape. He looked over at DAN. He was mimicking those around him, chanting, adding to the frenzy. Marcus so wanted to be an unfeeling machine like DAN at that moment. He did the only thing he could. He prayed for composure and strength.

The crowd quieted as the Beast entered through the dry ice mist. He strutted around the stage like a peacock and climbed to the podium. He abruptly raised his arms over his head with fists clenched. The crowd roared deafening approval. He opened his fist and slowly lowered his arms, and the noise subsided. He spoke directly into the cameras that were live streaming the event all over the world in every language. His tirade began.

"Citizens of Earth, you are privileged to be living in the greatest, most enlightened time the Earth has ever known. No longer do you need to worship a deity who cannot be seen or heard, or felt. I am all you need!" He raised his clenched fist and shook it in the air and the crowd responded with a loud roar. "I am announcing plans to rebuild the temple in Jerusalem where the Jews paid homage to that failed God of Abraham. My headquarters will be moved there upon completion of the structure. In less than a year, we will accomplish what took centuries for the Jews to do. From that place, I will reign over the entire world at piece, for no one is greater than the Beast and no one can fight him!"

Long adulation cheers erupted. He quieted the masses. "In two weeks, I will start an eradication program. Anyone clinging to the old ways and worshiping any god but the Beast will be gathered in this very arena and given a chance to bow to me.

If they refuse, they will be brought to the Justice of the Beast." His voice peaked with the crescendo roar of a lion. "A bounty of a month's supply of the glorious Amy will be awarded to anyone bringing in a dissenter."

The crowd whistled and roared. Again, he calmed them. He was planning his coming out party. In a few minutes, the crowd would witness the most gruesome sight since the Dracula of old walked the Earth.

"In keeping with the policies of peace and prosperity for all, the Beast will demonstrate what happens to the ones who get rich at the expense of my loyal subjects." The entrance to the floor of the stadium opened and eleven men were forced at gunpoint to enter. As the Beast's platform slowly lowered to the floor, he explained. "Before you are the last remnants of the drug traffickers in all of Egypt. They have exported their wares all over the world and caused untold suffering to all who are addicted. Tonight, for the entire world to see I will personally carry out their sentence."

Does he not see the irony in his statements! Marcus thought. He is the biggest drug dealer the world has ever seen. He knew before the Beast started that the men in the arena were doomed. He didn't know them but said a prayer for their souls.

The Beast approached the men, motioning them to take a weapon from the tables in front of them. The men grabbed the rifles and aimed them at the

Beast. DAN recorded the flight of the demons from the Beast to the men with his high-speed infra-red cameras. They stood like statues until the Beast allowed them to move. He lifted the nearest man in the air by the throat with one hand. He held the man high in the air and lifted his other hand as he circled around to address every section of the stadium. The man writhed and kicked, his hands clawing at his throat in an effort to breath. When the Beast had gone full circle, he put the man's face close to his so he could see and smell his dying fear. That was the best, the most potent. In the blink of an eye, the Beast palmed the man's head like a soccer ball with his free hand and, with the roar of a Beast for effect, lifted and twisted the man's head from his body. He discarded the body in a heap and rolled the head toward the goal like a bowling ball.

The stunned crowd fell silent. The Beast was oblivious as he grabbed the next man. The men had as much chance of fleeing or fighting the Beast as a toddler in a den of lions. He repeated the heinous act ten more times, cameras rolling his conquest all over the world.

After finishing the last one, he trotted over to where the heads stopped rolling and gave each a kick into the goal. The blood and fluids left in the sculls exploded out of every orifice, like an aura around each, as they traveled spinning through the air. As the last one bounced into the net, the

Beast turned to the crowd and raised his arms, fists clenched, and roared "Goaaallll!!"

The fear and anxiety in the stadium fed the Beast. Never before had he been on such a high. He grabbed the corpses one at a time by the feet and twirled them around like an ancient Olympian throwing a hammer. The blood and bodily fluids gushed out of the necks and splattered the crowds. When he let them fly, the corpses hit the protective net that usually kept overly exuberant fans from throwing debris onto the field. The bodies rolled back down onto the field. The frenzied Beast's roar echoed throughout the stadium.

"The God of Abraham may have created these wretched beings, but now I own their souls!" the Beast gloated, saying a prayer to his father, Satan.

Marcus was living his nightmare. He sat with his head buried in his hands, his eyes closed, hoping he would wake at any moment. DAN stood motionless, recording everything the Beast did.

The whole stadium fell deathly silent.

The Beast started a tirade of directives mostly at the Jews and Christians, blaming them for every problem created in the world. Hitler's speeches paled in comparison to the Beast.

The Beast knew that his audience was spell bound by fear. He used the emotion to plant his ideology deep into their psyche. Their souls and their minds belonged to him.

He left the podium. The soldiers held up signs that said applause in one hand and their weapons in the other. The crowd responded slowly at first but eventually a wave of noise rippled through the stadium. They were applauding out of fear.

The stadium started to empty. Marcus sat for a long time. He finally mustered the courage to get up and leave. DAN followed him as they exited the stadium in silence. Marcus had hoped he could distribute more fliers, but he felt he had to go home. When they were clear of the crowd, he reached in his vest pocket and touched the paper he carried. They would leave from the same place they arrived.

They followed the crowd into the subway to get across town to their temporary home. It was getting late, and Marcus was emotionally, physically, and spiritually spent. They rode in silence. Most everyone on the train was in shock from the spectacle of the Beast. Apartment four twenty-nine was a welcome haven after the long train ride. Marcus went straight to bed though he knew he wouldn't sleep. DAN sat in the chair, humming softly as he processed the data.

Marcus rose just before dawn and prepared to leave. He gathered the remaining papers and his few belongings. He kept thinking of the Jackal, his emaciated frame and the animal behavior. He found a bag and emptied the contents of the pantry. He had just enough room left in the bag for the partial loaf of bread on the counter. He nodded to DAN and they left the apartment. They had to get out of the area before the morning chaos.

The sun tweaked the top of the tall buildings as Marcus approached the Jackal's lair. He saw the man was still in his tent. The truck wouldn't be there for at least another hour, but he was already stirring. Marcus called him by the only name he knew, Jackal. The man burst out of his makeshift tent knife first. DAN was on high alert. Marcus offered the Jackal the bag of food. The man eyed it with lust. He wanted it with all his being, like a starving wild animal, but was fearful of accepting it. Marcus brought the bag closer.

"I don't need this anymore. I'd like you to have it." He took the bottle he purchased the night before and extended it to the Jackal. His need for Amy overwhelmed his caution and he grabbed the bag and the water.

His eyes said, "Why are you doing this for me?"

Then he turned and dove into his tent.

Marcus was not compelled to give the Jackal a paper, or an answer. He knew the man's soul was lost and that he just prolonged his agony with the gift of food, but God worked in miraculous ways. It was not up to him to judge. After what he had witnessed the night before, he had to do something no matter how small. He thought of the verse in Matthew 25:40. "What you do for the least of these, my brothers and sisters, you do for me. "

He walked around the corner to the rendezvous location with DAN and welcomed the soft light of the Eagle as the ramp lowered. He was going home.

18

Worldly Problems

The New World Order was not doing well. Chione, the Beast, the mysterious gentleman from the Trilateral, and the heads of state loyal to the Beast met in the Egyptian Parliament building they had commandeered for the occasion. The room was abuzz with different languages and cultures. Chione called for silence as she introduced the Beast. He rose to the podium. No press was allowed.

"I have done my part in uniting the world, but I have called this meeting at the request of the Trilateral to address the economic crisis looming on the horizon. I suggest you all find a way to fix it!"

Everyone in the room shuddered at the short but forceful speech. The Trilateral gentleman rose and addressed the gathering.

"We have witnessed the sharpest decline of wealth in the world history. Only one other time have we suffered this much loss, and we took care of that upstart Elias Tobias Montague. He thought he could bring us down by extorting a trillion bitcoin from us and redistributing it. He was short sighted in his plan. A trillion bitcoin is a few days' revenue for us. We recovered instantly and he paid for his transgressions with his life. This is different. We are facing a global downturn that we may not recover from. It is simple economics, the forces of supply and demand.

"In the last year, we have lost thirty-five percent of our global population. We can account for five percent; it was expected and was related to the amygdaloideum reaction, the accidents, and the increase in suicides caused by the drug. We cannot account for the other thirty percent. They've just vanished."

A man stood up from the American delegation. Chione recognized him.

"I am James Baker the Third from the world province formerly known as the United States of America. If you allow me the floor, I think I can answer your questions why the population has faltered."

"I come from a long line of preachers. My family has an uncanny knack of saying what the Christian people want to hear. We can open their pocket books to support a "ministry" that allows us to lead a lavish lifestyle."

Chione stood up, agitated. "Get to the point, Mr. Baker."

He nodded acknowledgement and continued, "You have essentially put us out of business. The churches are empty and closing. Most of the true Christians are gone. They have vanished into thin air. This is the demise of the Church as we know it.

"In America, we've been distributing Amy at cost in an attempt to keep our population compliant and productive. It hasn't worked. The ambition is gone; the drive that made us great has been washed away with Amy. Our country is bankrupt, and there is widespread rioting in the streets. Our warehouses are full, our factories silent. There are not enough people left to buy the goods produced."

"Where have they gone?" roared the Beast, fire in his eyes.

Baker continued, unfazed by the tirade, "My master is a scholar of the Bible, right? You know the teachings better than I do. Some interpret the rapture of the masses who follow Christ at the end of God's reign. This means that the believers will be protected by God in the end times. This has something to do with these papers."

He produced one of the silicon papers and gave it to a guard who handed it to the Beast. He turned it over in his hands and crumpled it like a discarded letter. The Beast glared at the American.

"The papers are found discarded everywhere," continued the man, trying to get his point across before the fury of the Beast peaked.

I found many of them in my church, and the next Sunday, no one came. I propose that we find someone who sees what is hidden in these papers and inject them with a tracking device and see where they go. No one would suspect me if I handed out these papers. I volunteer to get the information for the good of the New Order."

The Beast liked this brash subject from across the sea. He'd have to keep a close eye on the man, but no one else in the room offered any other explanation.

"If you succeed, you will have a high place in my kingdom!"

The American swallowed hard. He was taking a gamble, but he wanted to be on the winning side and this seemed to be it, at the moment. He bowed low to the Beast.

The Beast took the floor, "Since you have so much in your country, we will distribute it to the entire world!" declared the Beast.

The Trilateral gentleman cringed. The Beast knew nothing about world economics. Most businesses were owned by a few powerful families in the Trilateral in the guise of socialism. This was hurting the people whom the Beast needed to stay in power. He had to do something.

When the meeting dissipated, he approached Jim Baker and requested to have dinner with him. Mr. Baker got into the long black limousine that pulled to the curb.

The first thing Baker asked when he got into the limo was his name. "No one introduced you in the conference," he remarked.

"I seldom use my name. There are always the inquisitive ones who want to expose our little clique. I feel I can trust you. We are cut from the same cloth. We see the masses as an exclusive possession that is put on the Earth to serve us. Besides, if you cross me, you will meet the same fate as all the other social justice fanatics that have tried to bring us down. It's not usually a pleasant death."

"My name is J. P. Rothfellas the third. I am the culmination, so far, of selective breeding of the wealthiest families on the planet. I personally have been cloned three times. We have managed to keep our bloodline pure and our wealth intact since the dawn of the industrial age. We have waited a long time for this to happen, but some unforeseen things have transpired. Like the disappearance of so many people."

"I think the only solution is to start a war. We supply both sides of the conflict. Of course, the Beast will be the winner. He can then consolidate his power and rule indefinitely. We prosper, and you get a piece of the spoils. All you have to do is manipulate the outcome of your search. The individuals you tag must head for the Gaza strip, San Francisco in America, the Kremlin in Russia, and many other sites I have marked for destruction. We will make it seem like the ones responsible for the attack on the Beast are somehow congregated in those areas.

"While you are here, Mr. Baker, take in one of the Beast's rallies. The masses love him, well; they love Amy that sells so cheap in the stadium. The stadium is usually packed, but I have a pass for you in the VIP section. I'll also assign you some body guards. You never know when they might come in handy."

"Thank You, Mr. Rothfellas," Mr. Baker said. "I'll do that. Maybe we can manufacture a "Christian" to accomplish our goal. I'm looking forward to it."

"You will have my car at your disposal after dinner. Take in the show. Who knows, maybe you'll find who you are looking for."

19

Six-Six-Six

His plans to rebuild the temple in Jerusalem to its original glory were in full swing. In a month, it would stand gleaming white in the sun, as a monument to his success, not the God of Abraham. Not since King Solomon had the temple seen such glory. Sacrifices would resume just as in David's time but the blood would pay tribute his power. He would be the one and only God.

At the same time the sacrifices were to resume, a golden Image in the likeness of the Beast was to be unveiled in the newly built Temple of the Beast, its image broadcast all over the world by satellite, so everyone everywhere could bow down and worship it. The chip, the mark of the Beast introduced at his last rally, would be made available to everyone in the world. Chione and her Demonic cabinet of Enforcers had done a thorough job. The Beast was well pleased. He would reign in Jerusalem forever.

As suggested by J.P. Rothfellas and the Trilateral Commission, starting at the next rally, a universal chip would be implanted in the forehead or the wrist of every citizen of the realm. The chip was required to buy or sell anything in the Beast's New World. To refuse it meant death by beheading or starvation for those that managed to evade the Beast's police. Too many soldiers were getting rich by gouging the public for Amy. They presented a threat to the stability of the Beast's rule. More and more people were unable to pay their price. Most of the Beast's victims at his rallies now were these military leaders. They were a crowd's favorite. The chip would solve the black-market problem and allow the Realm to know everything about their subjects.

When his consolidation of power was complete, peace would reign throughout the world and everyone would bow down to him. He scheduled his last rally in the Egyptian stadium where he burst onto the world stage as the greatest soccer player to ever live. It now seemed beneath someone of his stature to hold these events. He would turn them over to Chione and her deputies to ensure total loyalty of his subjects.

20

The Jackal

The latest delivery of Amy had been fruitful for the Jackal. Since the stranger handed him the bag of food and the bottle of Amy, he had managed to keep ahead of the madness. As he lay in his tent staring into space, his mind wondered. He was once in line for CEO of the largest airline in the world until his treachery was discovered. He stepped on or eliminated many people and bought off many others to get that promotion. He had it locked up, or so he thought, but an informant exposed his treachery and his embezzlement to the board of directors.

His plea agreement got him off with five years in a minimum-security prison in Cairo. After his release, he roamed the streets of the city. One day, he came across a station that provided free bottles of water. He thought it was an advertising promotion so he took one. It was the worst mistake of his many mistakes in life.

Never trust anyone. Trust is what brought him down the first time. He always knew that someday he would claw his way back to the top, but this Amy thing had him whipped. He was at his lowest when the stranger with a weird companion handed him the food and the extra bottle of Amy.

The Jackal was at a loss to explain the man's actions. He mulled it over time after time, but couldn't fathom doing something like that without getting something in return. The next time, he would follow the man and learn the reason for his kindness.

Marcus and DAN were on their last mission. They were dropped off by the Eagle at the location where they met Steven and Sabella. According to the propaganda, this was the last rally for the Beast and it was urgent that they attend.

It was early morning when they walked by the Jackal's tent. They wanted to beat the delivery caravan and the crowd. The Jackal saw them stroll by. He watched them enter the building a few blocks down. After the delivery, he would sneak down there and see if he could find out more information on the man that gave him the food. For now, he had to worry about surviving another day.

21

Judas

The morning delivery is more civilized than usual, Marcus thought, peering through the window at the gathering below. Though barbaric, the Beast's measures did have an impact on the population. They no longer had to choose between food, shelter, and Amy. He caught a glimpse of the Jackal as he dove back into his tent for his morning ritual.

Marcus wondered about him and even prayed for him on occasion. He wondered if the gift he gave him had any kind of impact.

That's the trouble with random acts of kindness; the outcome is only for God to know. Marcus mused as he watched the activity wind down below. They had a few hours to kill before they had to catch the train to the stadium.

Marcus had his recurring dream last evening about the stadium. He hadn't had it since he started his mission to distribute the silicon papers. He was very frightened at first, but a presence appeared in his room and calmed his fear. He was at peace. He did not know what lay in store for him, but he was sure he wouldn't return to his sanctuary in the mountain.

He envied DAN whose mission was clear. He had been modified in the last months and was now a killing machine. The sensors in his hand had been replaced by lasers. His machine reflexes could fry a fly in flight at fifty meters. The drawback to his weapon was he had one shot, and it took many seconds to recharge the laser.

Marcus was ninety percent positive that DAN could complete his mission alone, but the uncertain ten percent compelled him to volunteer for the mission. They had one shot at saving humanity, and he wanted to ensure success.

Midafternoon, they left for the train to the stadium without realizing they were being stalked. The Jackal waited for them down the block hidden in a shadowy alley, next to the sign posted by the police that read, "A bounty of a month's supply of Amy to anyone who brings in a dissenter that refuses to bow down to the Beast. Two month's supply for turning in a professing Christian."

The Jackal followed them into the train. He didn't have a pass or a bit-card, but that never stopped him before. He knew how to beat the system; after all, he had been doing it all his life. The Jackal positioned himself so he could see Marcus and DAN.

Of course, thought the Jackal, they were going to the rally. He exited the train lost in the surge of humanity.

When they went through the gate, he watched the direction they took. It would take him a little while to breach this security. He ran around the block where a shipment of Amy was being unloaded. The troops guarding Amy recruited anyone off the street to unload the shipments, usually at gunpoint, so they wouldn't have to do it themselves. He purposely made himself conspicuous.

A soldier pointed his weapon at him. "You! Come here!"

The Jackal complied.

"Start unloading this truck!" the soldier commanded.

The Jackal walked toward the truck to get in the procession of workers going into and out of the building like ants.

"Not so fast!" The soldier blocked his path. "Turn around."

When the Jackal complied, the soldier stamped a number on the back of his cloak and pushed him toward the line with the butt of his weapon.

Since the reign of the Beast, it seemed society was headed backward. A short time ago, androids would have taken care of this mundane task. No matter, it was a way for him to gain access.

He queued up to take a box.

"Follow the line," the soldier commanded.

The Jackal nodded and followed. By his second trip, he had a plan. When he put down his box, he nudged the guy next to him, causing the workers to stumble domino style. In the ensuing chaos, the guards scrambled to restore dominance and order. He made his move. He stripped off his coat, wadded it in front of him, and casually walked toward the service entrance tunnel to the stadium with the other workers arriving for the event. He stashed his garment in the first trash can and ducked in the first open door. He heard the guards cursing the men involved in the altercation. He waited until the furor died down. He slinked from place to place, each move getting him closer to his goal.

One of the doors was a storeroom for maintenance items. He rummaged through the uniforms on the wall and found one that fit. He was now on the maintenance staff. He grabbed a broom and dustpan for props and made his way to the last place he saw the two benefactors he pursued.

It was an hour before the rally, so the crowd was not at full capacity. Most were milling around buying souvenirs of the Beast's last rally or bottles of water. Since the Beast started his campaign to stop the price gouging by his own military, the seats in the stadium were filled by anyone his minions could gather and bus in from anywhere in the city. They knew that empty seats could cost them their life.

The Jackal systematically scanned every section of the stadium to locate his prey. He moved from section to section and pretended to sweep all while scanning the seats. In the middle section of the lower deck, he spotted two men calmly sitting next to a support pillar.

When he was a few rows away, he knew for sure they were the ones. He pretended to clean the row below them. When he was close to them, he turned to face the one who gave him the Amy and the food.

Marcus didn't recognize the Jackal at first. He was out of his environment and didn't have on his signature trench coat with the pockets he used to gather the Amy.

DAN said, "Jackal," and Marcus recognized him.

Before he could speak, the Jackal blurted, "Why did you give me the stuff?"

Marcus gazed into the man's eyes and knew the reason he was so compelled to give him the food and water. He was staring at his Judas.

A peace washed over him, and with a knowing smile, he told the Jackal boldly, "We are Christians and that is what we are commissioned by God to do for brothers in need."

"Without getting anything in return?"

"Our reward is stored in Heaven waiting on our arrival."

The Jackal didn't have a clue what Marcus was talking about. Without even a thank you, he moved on. He carried on his charade until he reached the stadium landing. He ditched the broom and headed straight for security. This was his ticket back to the top. With that much Amy he could concentrate on getting ahead instead of keeping alive.

He approached the first guard he saw. "I've got some information your boss should hear."

"Yeah, right! Why don't you tell me and I'll be the judge?"

"I've got information there are two Christians here tonight. I'm sure that information would make the Beast happy."

"I'll relay the information to him."

"You take me for an idiot? If I tell you, you'll kill me and take the glory and Amy for yourself! I want assurances!"

The guard pondered for a while before answering the Jackal. If I don't act and this guy is telling the truth, I'm as good as dead, but if the guy was a deranged idiot, I'll be the laughing stock of his unit. Better a live idiot.

"Come with me," he said.

They both went to head security where the Jackal repeated his story. The Jackal was surrounded by police, menacing him, threatening him. He didn't waiver. When Gustaf, the head of security, was finally convinced, he commanded his men to guard the Jackal with their lives. If what the man said was true, the Beast would be thrilled. He entered the chambers of the Beast.

After what seemed like an eternity, Gustaf reemerged and motioned the Jackal to enter. The

Jackal swallowed hard and went into his act. As soon as he entered, he fell prostrate at his host's feet.

The Beast looks larger and more intimidating in person than on the screen, the Jackal thought, trembling.

He regained his composure and gushed. "My Lord! What an honor to be in your presence!"

Without any acknowledgement, the Beast looked him in the eye and growled, "So you have information on two Christians here tonight?"

"Yes, Lord," he said without hesitation. "I believe there is a bounty for them."

"How do I know what you say is true?"

"I was in my tent minding my own business when one of them handed me a sack of food and a bottle of Amy. I couldn't believe he would do such a thing without getting anything in return so I followed him and his friend here tonight and asked them. They told me to my face they are Christians just a few minutes ago right here in your stadium."

The Jackal felt himself suspended by the throat. A guttural bear growl came out of the face centimeters from his. He could have sworn the Beast sniffed him like a bear would its prey. He trembled.

"See that the man gets his bounty if what he says is true. If he cannot find them, then add him to the show tonight. He'll make a fitting sacrificial example to anyone that crosses me!"

The Beast released his grip and the Jackal fell, gasping for breath at the Beast's feet. The guards grabbed him by the collar and drug him from the room.

"This better not be a scam, or I'll kill you myself!" threatened Gustaf.

The Jackal did his best to make up for the lost oxygen and could only nod and motion for the guard to follow. When they passed security stations, Gustaf motioned for the men to follow. Six guards in all took up positions to block the rows above and below Marcus and DAN. All the people in the seats in their row and in the rows above and below were motioned to leave by the brandishing of the guard's weapons. It was only Marcus, DAN, and security. The Jackal watched at a safe distance.

Not wanting to take any chances, the head guard positioned himself in front of the two and motioned with his weapon for them to stand.

"Are you Christians?" he asked, fully expecting them to deny it. After all, what idiot would voluntarily come into the enemy's lair like this?

They must be some kind of stupid if they answer yes, he pondered.

"Yes, we are Christians." Marcus stated, looking the man in the eye, steady, unafraid.

The little degenerate was right, the guard mused, as he ordered them handcuffed and led away.

The Jackal exhaled. He couldn't believe that these men would confess without being tortured or beaten. He couldn't believe his luck. By the end of the night, he would have enough of new Amy as collateral to find some new scam. He was back! All they had to do was refuse to bow to the Beast, and he could go home free.

The Beast was notified of the events. Marcus and DAN were scheduled as the finale to the Beast's gruesome show.

Gustaf led the Jackal to the area where Amy was stored and ordered his guards to portion off a four month's supply separately from the rest. The Jackal was overwhelmed. He hadn't thought through the logistics of getting that much water out of the stadium by himself. It would be impossible to carry alone and it would cost him dearly to hire help. He sat pondering his dilemma. Gustaf smiled an evil smile as he ordered all but one of his guards to get back to their posts.

Gustaf gave the remaining guard instructions to release the Amy to the Jackal only if Marcus and DAN didn't bow to the Beast. The Jackal paced the floor, sweating anxiously, looking for a way out of his dilemma. His heart pounded in his chest and time stood still.

22

A Theatrical Demise

Marcus and DAN were led down the corridor that used to be reserved for the football players. It was lined with condemned men. Some of them sat motionless while others whimpered softly. The duo was shoved down at the back end of the procession still in the handcuffs. A guard wrapped some chains around them and padlocked the ends together for effect. They would be a sight when they were shoved out into the arena.

Marcus began to pray loudly for them all. The guard used the butt of his weapon on Marcus' head to silence him when some of the men protested. The Beast's speech blared over the loudspeaker.

"I am introducing you to the future tonight. To eliminate any more graft or corruption, I will now require that all of my loyal subjects take what I have named the mark of the Beast. It's a chip implanted in the forehead or the right wrist with a mark of compliance. With this chip, any individual can buy or sell any goods or services in the realm. Everyone in this stadium will be marked before they can leave."

What he didn't say is that now every move of these poor souls can be tracked by the evilest ruler the world has ever known! Marcus thought. *There is no escape.*

"Now without delay we will start the tribunal. Chione, introduce the subjects and the charges of the first group."

Again, the loudspeakers blared.

"First Sergeant Arin Menassa, the first squad, in charge of water distribution for southeast quadrant of Cairo. Charges include extortion from the people of the Realm regarding the price charged for the goods in their care. What do you say, people of the world?"

The Beast raised his arms and the crowd started chanting, "Death! Death! Death!"

He raised his hands higher with palms out and the crowd silenced.

"I am going to make an example of these men. I'm going to show you all how much confidence I have in my mark of the Beast. I'm going to pardon these men. All they have to do is bow before me in tribute and be the first to take the mark."

The men couldn't believe they would be spared. Instantly, they fell prostrate before him. The guards dragged them to the machines set around the floor of the stadium and pushed their foreheads against the front of the machine. The instant the flesh touched the protruding bar, the chip was implanted and the mark of the Beast, 666, appeared on their foreheads.

Camera close-ups broadcast the event all over the world as one group of condemned after the other was pardoned and given the mark. Only Marcus and DAN were left in the corridor. The procedure dragged on as everyone in the seats was ushered down to the floor to give tribute to the Beast and receive the mark.

Finally, the people in the stands were seated again. The Beast then announced the final event, "People of the Glorious One, all powerful and knowing One, God of the world!"

A roar erupted from the crowd. The Beast raised his hands and took in the adulation. He calmed them with the wave of his hand.

"I have one more surprise tonight. I thought I had eradicated every Christian on the Earth, but tonight we have two who profess the banned religion. I will give them one chance to bow to me and take the mark. If they refuse, I will make examples of them. No one can resist the Beast!"

The crowd chanted, "Beast! Beast! Beast!"

Marcus and DAN were led to the arena floor to boos and jeers. The ones seated along the corridor spat on them and threw trash at them as they entered. The chains dragged along behind them, gleaming in the stadium light.

When they reached the middle of the arena, the guard took off the chains and handcuffs. The roar was deafening. Marcus and DAN stared straight ahead.

The Beast descended to the arena floor. The crowd's frenzy grew more rabid with anticipation. He walked casually over to them and greeted them like old friends. He raised his hand for silence.

When the arena was still, he spoke directly to Marcus. "You profess to be Christian. That is an automatic death sentence, but since I am in such a benevolent mood, I'm going to allow you and your partner to live. All you need to do is renounce your worthless God and bow on your knees to me."

"Never," Marcus said quietly, looking the Beast directly in the eyes.

The Beast's rage burst forth. His demons unleashed to keep his other prey in check until his time. Finding no soul in DAN, the demons entered the guards standing behind him paralyzing them. In his fury, the Beast didn't notice.

He lifted Marcus by the throat with one hand and swung him around for the whole crowd to see. They were in a frenzy again. Conditioned by all the blood and death at the Beast's performances, and savoring the possibility of Christian blood, they were on their feet.

The Beast was enjoying the ruse of being benevolent tonight. He let Marcus down and gave him another chance.

"Bow and worship me!"

"Never!" Marcus gasped with his last breath.

DAN was analyzing every move the Beast made, looking for the one instance when he could fire his lethal weapon but found no opportunity. Lazers are wonderful weapons at close range, but distort in atmospheric anomalies like the dry Ice haze that the Beast used at every performance for surreal effect. DAN calculated the probabilities of a kill shot were very slim, except at close range.

The Beast lifted Marcus again and brought him close to smell his fear but found none.

Marcus' soul floated above the carnage when his head left his body. He felt peace instead of pain; he was in the presence of his Lord.

The Beast swung his body around. Marcus' blood spilled red on all the close bystanders and up into the stands. The Beast hung the body upside down on a cable like a side of beef in a meat locker and gave it a mighty shove. It swung around the stadium like it was flying. The Beast got tired of the spectacle. He was enraged by the lack of fear in these Christians.

He turned to DAN and lifted him off the stadium floor. When his eyes stared into DAN's, he realized something was wrong. DAN didn't grasp at his throat. Instead, he unleashed his laser point blank at the right side of the Beast's face.

The mighty Beast fell to the same stadium floor where he had seen so much glory and adulation as a player, and as the leader of the New World.

A stunned hush fell over the stadium. No one could process what had just happened. DAN jumped on the platform that carried the Beast and began to rise.

Marcus' remains swung hideously in ever decreasing circles directly over the lifeless Beast in a morbid revenge.

DAN knew he was never getting out of the stadium. It wasn't in the plan. When the crowd recovered from the shock of seeing their invincible leader on the floor, the guards opened fire with total disregard for the people trapped in the stadium. Screams of agony and panic rocked the air. The guns wailed; laser bursts rained in every direction like a hurricane driven rain.

The stands ran red with the blood of the Beast's loyal subjects. Those not hit by the lasers were trampled in the carnage of people trying to flee.

Some of the lasers were hitting their intended target. DAN was halfway up in the platform waiting for his laser to recharge. Pieces of his android body were tearing away. At last, his sensors indicated full charge. He turned the lasers on himself and fired.

The composite material he was made of exploded with the fury of a large fireworks display, spewing white hot shrapnel into the flesh of many survivors.

The stench of their own burning hair and flesh seared their nostrils, adding to the agony.

The position of the platform spared the Beast from the fallout. Security finally regained control of the remainder of the crowd. The victims were left to their agony while the available paramedics tended to the Beast.

Chione watched in disbelief from her broadcast suite as everything she worked on for centuries slipped away. Gustaf would pay for his breach of security, but right now he was still useful.

She summoned him, "tell the paramedics to bring the Beast here to my suite. We cut the broadcast before the carnage but not before the attack on the Beast. We can't afford to let out any more information until I consult with my master."

After Gustaf left, Chione paced the room.

The stretcher arrived with the body of the Beast.

She caressed the Beast's limp hand, tears streaming down her face as the paramedic delivered the bad news.

"We've stabilized his pulse and breathing by artificial means. We need to get him immediately to the nearest neurosurgery hospital. We can't find any signs of brain activity."

"Then get him there, NOW!" she screamed.

They double timed him to the ambulance as the guards cleared a path through the confused mob.

She prayed to her dark master, summoning his strength and wisdom. She stood trembling while the mist permeated the room. She felt the jolt as the Evil One entered her presence. She fell to her knees, then prostrate.

"Master, what must I do?" she prayed.

She came out of the room an hour later with eyes blazing red and evil in her aura.

She ordered Gustaf to enter the room. He shook in the presence of the evil.

"Write this down because I'm only going to say it once. I am making you totally responsible for the events that transpired here tonight. The only redemption for you is to follow my instructions to the letter.

Gustaf took out his phone and started recording. His hands were visibly shaking with fear and grief.

"Take the fastest transport jet to Russia's Red Square and bring me the glass tomb of Lenin and get it to Jerusalem."

"But what should I do with Lenin's body?" he asked.

I don't care what you do with that wax figurine. Just get me the sarcophagus now!"

The fire in her eyes and the tone in her voice told him he was one second away from oblivion, so he saluted and left.

23

Jackal's Justice

The Jackal sat on cases of the Amy and pondered over his plight. Just as he was about to take what he could carry and leave the rest; a group of soldiers entered the storeroom. He didn't recognize the symbol on their uniforms. It was a triangle with some sort of emblem on every point and a big "T" embossed in the center.

A well-dressed man strolled through the ranks and came up to the Jackal to introduce himself. "My name is James Baker the Third. We are a part of the Beast's regime not very well known to the populace called the Trilateral Commission. We operate below the radar, as they used to say. We may be able to help each other. Right now, these gentlemen are at your disposal to load your bounty onto a waiting refrigerated truck and transport it to wherever you wish, with your permission, of course."

The Jackal was very skeptical. Because of his own actions, he didn't trust easily, but he had no choice. He nodded and the men put down their weapons, loaded the carts, and wheeled some of the same Amy that the Jackal had helped unload earlier back onto a truck. He followed the last of his treasure out into the street.

He was about to get into the truck when a long black limo with the same emblem on the side pulled in beside him. The door opened, and Baker motioned the Jackal to get in. He glanced at his stash in the back of the truck still unsure of the circumstance. He reluctantly climbed in.

"Where to?" asked Mr. Baker.

The Jackal hesitated. He didn't have a clue how to answer. As soon as the Jackal was introduced as the man who brought in the two Christians, the security now at Mr. Baker's disposal, checked him out. He knew everything about the Jackal and his past life and devised a plan to exploit his greed. Baker was going to con the con man.

"I have a suite nearby where we can spend the night and formulate a plan of action," Baker said. "It has a secure garage for your water and the security men at your disposal." He anticipated the Jackal's next question. "You need to know what I want in return for my trouble? Very astute. We think alike, Mr. Simian Batiste."

The Jackal hadn't used that name since he got out of prison. He didn't know anyone knew it. "How do you know my name?" he asked.

"The Trilateral Commission knows everything it needs to know, Mr. Batiste. To answer your anticipated question, I have a business proposition for you. We need someone of your talents to convince people that Christians are behind all the government's problems. All the commotion you heard today was because one of the two Christians shot the Beast directly in the head with a very powerful laser. The Beast is dead, Mr. Batiste, and you are being held responsible. Your life is worthless on the streets, and I am your only hope."

"What should I do?" the Jackal asked.

"Simple. Like it or not, you are forever linked to the Christians. We are going to exploit that fact. You will carry a homing device into the southern part of former Israel to a designated spot, then to many other spots. Then you will leave the device at the designated areas and leave. You will be starting the conflicts in the world designed to balance the supply and demand problem. We are building a case for the largest police action the world has ever seen. Our operatives will be tracking you the entire journey.

"Once we establish a Christian or dissident settlement there, armies will surround the area and wipe out the threat. The people in harm's way will be forewarned of the attack and armed accordingly. With a little planning, the conflict will grow to a global scale. For your trouble, you will receive a life-time supply of Amy, a stipend of a million bit-coin a year, and a villa anywhere in the world you wish.

"If you refuse our generous offer, we will deposit your Amy anywhere you desire and never contact you again, but that also means you will be at the mercy of the Beast's police who, as we speak, have put a generous bounty on your head."

Baker smiled inwardly. The Jackal was a two-bit con man out of his league. If he had done his home-work, he would have known that the Amy he now possessed would be useless in less than a month. It was so unstable it had to be delivered daily in refrigerated trucks. Of course, he would help Mr. Batiste out and use the Amy as a political tool to gather favor with the right people.

The Jackal knew he had no choice in the matter. He had stumbled on a situation out of his control. He was a pawn in the deadliest chess game that man had ever known. Still, he would enjoy the good life, and it would be better than no life.

He extended his right hand to Mr. Baker. Baker shook it with a smile. No matter what, the Jackal would be dealt with when the time came.

"We have a room for you," he said. "You will find a change of clothes and a hot bath waiting. When you are ready, we will have dinner to finalize our plans.

The Jackal felt drawn to Baker's charm. He could survive even if they double crossed him. He knew how to milk the situation until it changed.

The Jackal was escorted to his quarters. His personal butler opened the door into an opulent room fit for a king. He was speechless. The butler led him to his sleeping quarters. On the bed was a very expensive suit in his size. In the master bath the water was running in the biggest bathtub he had ever seen. The towels were laid out and the fragrance of the lit candles filled the moist air. The butler bowed and left the room.

When the Jackal was done, he donned a bathrobe and walked into the bedroom. Waiting for him was a hair stylist and a manicurist who, together, would turn him into a different man. His scruffy beard was shaved, his hair cut and styled, and years of dirt were removed from his nails. They left him to get dressed for his dinner date with destiny.

Baker didn't recognize the Jackal when he walked into the restaurant. That was the idea, to keep him from being readily recognized by the photos being circulated over the media.

The android server escorted the Jackal to Mr. Baker's table as instructed.

"Welcome, Mr. Batiste. Please sit. May I call you Simian?"

The Jackal was impressed. It had been many years since anyone had given him the respect he thought he deserved.

"Call me Mr. Batiste," he answered, milking the moment for all it was worth.

"Very well, Mr. Batiste. Once you order, I will get down to business. I heard the lobster is excellent."

"I'm allergic to all seafood. I swell up like a balloon!"

Mr. Baker took note of that bit of information. He was sure the Trilateral knew it, but he wanted to be thorough. After the Jackal ordered, they got down to business.

"The reason we need your services, Mr. Batiste, is to eradicate once and for all the threat the Christian and other dissident population pose to the New World Order. We know they are out there, but we don't know where. We think you have inside information and are willing to share it. It was genius on your part to get the two that killed the Beast into the arena and down on the floor with him."

Baker knew greed and self-preservation motivated the Jackal above everything else and was about to exploit that fact.

If I tell him the truth, this scam might go away, the Jackal thought.

"Hey, I just have a knack for spotting them," He offered as a half-truth. "They were already there in the arena. I was being a good citizen and pointing them out like the Beast wanted. I didn't have a clue that they were going to do that."

"So, you don't know exactly where they are, but you can spot them when you see them." Mr. Baker played along. "We have intelligence that gives us a general area, but we don't know exactly where to search. With your expertise, we could pinpoint their location and save a lot of innocent lives when we go after them."

"Yeah, that's what I'm saying! If you get me close to a settlement, I can pinpoint it for you." The Jackal lied, but only out of one side of his mouth. The other side was full of food.

"Very good, Mr. Batiste. I think we can do some business. All you have to do is leave the tracking device as close to the settlements as you can, and we will do the rest. A personal jet will be at your disposal in the morning. We will give you the general area our intelligence suspects, and your unique talents can do the rest. There are ten locations in all. Keep in touch." And with that Baker excused himself and left the Jackal to his meal.

• • •

The Trilateral people were very thorough. One of the buttons in his new outfit was a homing device. Since he didn't have the mark of the Beast, they alone could track the Jackal after he delivered the "official" device that would convince the world that a Christian settlement was in former south Israel, as well as other strategic locations around the world.

The Jackal would deliver the "proof" they needed and with a little planning, the whole world would be at war in a month.

What a timely circumstance, thought Baker.

• • •

The Jackal was indeed living the high life. He jetted all over the world planting the evidence. He didn't go through security or stand in line. Presidents were not privy to the treatment he enjoyed, but all good things come to an end.

He decided after the last location was targeted, that he would settle in a penthouse suit in Las Vegas, Nevada, the Sodom and Gomorrah of his dreams, as far away from home as possible.

He had "his people" take care of the details. He hit the casino the minute he stepped out of the taxi.

After a night of gambling, he went to his penthouse and had breakfast catered. "His" people were actually part of the "cleanup committee" for the Trilateral. His meal was laced with a substance known to trigger anaphylactic shock in people with any seafood allergies.

The Jackal had overestimated his worth. his throat tightened, causing him to stagger onto the balcony gasping for air. Clandestine eyes watched as he struggled for life.

The neon skyline of the city reflected in his glazed eyes. Was that the last image he saw on this earth, or was it the pavement rushing toward him?

The door to his suite closed softly as the attendant wheeled away the remains of the tampered meal and any link to foul play. To the outside world, he looked like just another distraught gambler unable to face his losses. He landed on the street face down.

24

The Resurrection Deception

Gustaf and his men jumped out of the huge helicopter as it landed in Red Square. A crew had been ordered to remove the giant glass sarcophagus that held Lenin for so many centuries.

One butcher for another, Gustaf thought to himself. The Beast hadn't murdered the millions Lenin had, but it was only a matter of time. Guess that won't happen now. A wry smile crossed his lips. His own life was precarious at best since the Beast's demise. He knew he was at the mercy Chione. As soon as he was no longer useful to her, she would exterminate him like so many others. He was a soldier, born to follow orders no matter what. He would carry out his mission and deliver the tomb.

It was clear in Chione' mind, the "Miracle" that was about to be seen by millions. The Beast was indeed brain dead but only temporarily. Satan had a plan. His body would go on display in Lenin's glass tomb in Jerusalem's temple. There was no time to construct one, but Lenin's tomb could be fashioned into a hyperbolic chamber to keep the Beast alive and healing.

As soon as the mist left her, she ordered paramedics, along with the best doctors, to transport the Beast's body to Jerusalem when the sarcophagus arrived. She convened a meeting of all the staff involved in the running of the Beast's empire to let them know about the plan. While the doctors and engineers worked to secure the body in its tomb and provide the environment to keep the Beast alive, she filled in the elite on their roll.

"We have a dire situation here. The Beast is indeed brain dead but I've consulted our master. Satan has a plan to use this to solidify the worship of the Beast. When all is ready and the Beast's body is secured in his temporary tomb, the master is going to heal his affliction. He will rise from the dead in three days. We need to make sure thousands are visiting the tomb and millions are watching on the monitors. We will turn this setback into the greatest spectacle of all time and squelch the opposition. He will truly be worshiped."

She addressed the minister of propaganda and tasked him, threatened him, with making sure everyone would mourn the Beast.

"A constant stream of mourners must walk past the coffin," she commanded. "Thousands will be present, day and night, for the cameras. He will be positioned so the wounds are minimized to the viewers and the cameras. Use lighting, holography, or magic, anything to assure his dignity. I want the most solemn, sad procession the world has ever seen so when the resurrection takes on the third day the impact will be colossal!"

Gustaf arrived and sat in on the proceedings at Chione's request.

"I want guards to keep order at all times. No one should be allowed within five meters of the casket." She glared fire from her eyes at Gustaf.

He nodded and bowed in compliance. Another assignment meant life for a little longer. He slipped out of the meeting to begin coordinating his men immediately.

He surveyed the grounds to formulate a schedule for the officers. The area where the Beast's body would lie was bathed in an eerie, artificial light. The technicians were using a live subject to check lighting effects inside the casket. The man sat up just as Gustaf walked by. Reflex fast his gun was drawn and aimed at the tech in the casket. Thankfully, Gustaf hesitated long enough to analyze the situation before opening the fire. He was shaking, his adrenalin at its peak. The tech was busy checking his data and was clueless to his brush with death.

At least I showed the proper restraint. What a day! Worse day of my life and it isn't over! Thought Gustaff.

When the lighting and security were established, the doctors wheeled the gurney carrying the Beast to the glass enclosure. Everyone except Gustaf and the doctors were hustled out of the area. They eased the Beast into his resting place. All the IVs were hidden and the tomb sealed with a constant oxygen-rich controlled climate. Gustaf had an uneasy feeling as they positioned his ruler for the optimum visual effect. The mourners would arrive in the morning, but for now Gustaf would provide a lone vigil. His men were stationed on a pre- established perimeter outside of the temple area.

At midnight, Chione strolled in alone. Gustaf didn't recognize her at first and approached her from the side with his weapon ready.

"At least you can do something right!" she said.

The red fire of her eyes stopped him in his tracks. He felt a presence, a force field, an evil that paralyzed him. He saw her lay both hands on the glass and dark mists engulf her and the Beast. An evil threatened to rip his soul from his body. Terror seemed to sweat from every pore. His mind's eye saw the Beast savoring his fear. He expected that any moment his head would be ripped from his body, like he'd witnessed in the arena.

A movement in the tomb caught his eye. The Beast convulsed, suspended in space. Gustaf was sure he saw a second entity with the Beast.

He woke in a heap. Chione left, and the tomb became silent. The ghostly light gave the Beast an illusion of normal sleep. Gustaf fought off the threatening madness by reaching for that ever-present flask. He gulped the laced water within without hesitation, waiting for the drug to enter his brain and take away the pain.

Moments later, he commanded his men to open the barriers for the multitude of mourners gathered outside. They were promised a bottle of Amy in honor of the Beast. Only the undamaged side of the Beast's head was visible to them, and they were kept five meters away from the glass.

The message over the giant screens read, "Honor the Beast by getting the mark."

The mourners complied after walking past the glass coffin. They all talked in hushed tones about the fate of the one World Government and what would happen to them now.

The main topic was would the supply of Amy continue? Rumors were already circulating about the armies amassing all over the world to fight the Christian menace.

The sun rose and set as it always did, but there was darkness in the world. The one who promised world peace and endless prosperity was lying dead in a borrowed coffin.

For the billions of people who couldn't attend the actual viewing, the event was broadcast all over the world. Everywhere, commerce stood still and all activities, except distribution of the Amy and receiving the mark, ceased.

The steady stream of mourners continued into the second day. When the viewing public peaked on the third day, the dark mist started to permeate the glass enclosure until the Beast was no longer visible inside.

The crowd froze, watching the glass intently. No one breathed. The mist turned from dark red to black, swirling in its confinement. The glass exploded, pieces pelting the crowd and causing the closest bystanders to be blown backward. Their blood stained the new floor.

A roar went up from the crowd. There was the Beast, sitting on the edge of the tomb. He rose through the remaining mist, arms raised. The crowd recovered and fell prostrate in worship. He was truly a God!

Chione watched from her headquarters where she had orchestrated everything. A smile crossed her face for the first time in three days. The events leading to the "resurrection "played right into the Beast's hands. No one would question that he was indeed God! No one would be able to oppose him now.

Who can fight the Beast! She thought, giddy with her power.

He wobbled slightly and seemed disoriented. Gustaf ordered his men to roll out the throne in the temple that was going to be unveiled during the upcoming sacrifices planned for the next week. They discreetly helped the Beast into the golden throne bordered with every precious stone imaginable in a gaudy display of his self-appointed position. It was bordered with black diamonds around a crest that had "The Beast" emblazoned in white pearl above his head. The golden arm rests fit him perfectly. The golden swirls at the end of the arm rests caressed his powerful hands down to his fingerprints. Not since Solomon reined was there such a display of power and wealth.

Maybe Chione would keep this Gustaf around. He seemed to have a natural ability to rise to the occasion. However, her joy was short-lived.

She noticed the unsteady confusion of the Beast. The live worldwide feed had to be delayed until they could edit the footage. The Beast could not show any weakness in his moment of triumph.

25

A Miracle?

G ustaf and his men thrust their weapons repeatedly in the air, driving the crowd into a frenzy like cheerleaders. The Beast raised his right arm and waved to the crowd weakly. Gustaf and his cronies slowly rolled the throne back and lowered the veil of the Tabernacle, trying to convey pomp and power in the process.

As soon as the curtain touched the floor, the Beast wilted, slithering out of his throne like a drunk sliding off a barstool. A team of the best doctors in the world was standing by to examine him. The paramedics stabilized him and whisked him off to the hospital.

Days of testing followed. Considering the severity of his brain damage, it was remarkable that he could still function at all. He was blind and deaf on his right side. His head pounded and a bright light seemed to blind him, even in the dark, for minutes at a time. The wound would get extensive plastic surgery and the flesh would heal, but the damage to his psyche was irreparable.

His security team betrayed him. His loyal subjects failed him. Satan, his father, was a destroyer, not a healer. Satan was incapable of restoring him to his rightful glory. The Beast slipped into a dark depression.

The doctors, afraid for their lives, gave him any drug he demanded. Chione was furious but couldn't persuade him to leave the drugs alone. He had his moments of sanity before the painkillers wore off, and the hallucinogenic drugs took over.

Chione called a meeting of the high command that kept order over the vast empire to brief them on the health of the Beast. As she had her whole life, she would do her master's bidding. Mr. Rothfellas would attend. He brought along his assistant, Mr. Baker, to present at the summit the evidence for war. It seemed, with the assassination attempt, their timing was perfect.

Before all the delegates assembled, he met separately with Mr. Baker to finalize the plans to eradicate all the Christian population from the face of the earth.

"Did you get our strategy mapped out to present at the summit, Mr. Baker?" he asked.

"Yes, sir. Mr. Batiste marked all the sites you specified before meeting his sudden death in Las Vegas," Mr. Baker said with a wry smile. "I believe he jumped off a balcony in a moment of despondence because he couldn't pay a gambling debt."

"How unfortunate!" Sarcasm dripped from Rothfellas' words.

"We have every location mapped like you requested. I have one question. I thought the Christians were gone. How am I to convince the council otherwise?"

"That is your problem, Mr. Baker. Call them Christians, Muslims, dissidents, whatever. They fell through the cracks. They are either unaffected by the Amy or never ingested it. They refuse the mark of the Beast so that makes them his enemies. We are doing the Beast a favor by eradicating them. It should be a short but profitable war. The outnumbered and outgunned rebels will fall shortly."

Baker was uncomfortable with his superior's attitude. Underestimating an opponent, no matter how outgunned, was bad strategy in his book. Besides, it was his neck on the line, not Rothfellas', if he set in motion this war and things didn't go as planned. He knew how ruthless his new boss could be.

They got in the black limo waiting at the curb and rode in silence. Baker mentally went over his presentation. By week's end, the whole world would be at war if his presentation went well. They exited the limo at the summit and took their seat on the podium at the right of Chione.

The rest of the council entered in single file and took their seats around the opulent conference table facing the delegates. The usual din accompanied the gathering until Chione rose to speak. The room fell silent.

"The New World Order suffered a severe setback when the Beast was attacked and killed. Thanks to our Master Satan for restoring him to us on the third day. Although he is again among the living, it will be a long road of recovery for him."

She was lying. She didn't know if he would ever recover completely, but she had a plan. Only his personal doctors and security team knew the true condition of the Beast, and they were sworn to silence.

"From now on, the Beast will only address his subjects at the front of the temple behind the curtain. We have the latest holographic equipment, and the best technicians working on a method of presenting the Beast as restored. A golden image of him will stand in the entrance of the temple for all to worship. His image will seem to come out of the golden likeness and address the crowd. After his speech, he will seem to disappear into a mist absorbed by the golden image."

She continued, "We need total domination of the people. As you will hear later in a presentation, we have a plan to eradicate the opposition to the New World Order. We need each and every one of you to get the mark of the Beast installed in every citizen of the realm in the next two weeks. After that time, the people who refuse will be considered our enemies and will be eradicated. Mr. Baker from the Trilateral will give us a briefing on the progress of the investigation to find and bring to justice the ones responsible for the attack on the Beast. Mr. Baker, you have the floor."

He nodded and rose to the podium. Something happened to him when he got up to address a crowd. The power he felt when in control of an audience was his drug of choice. By the time he was through with this crowd, there would be no question that war was the only solution.

"Esteemed colleagues, I assure you that this heinous act of treason will not go unpunished. There were three directly involved. Two were killed on the day of the attack, and the third one met his demise at his own hands, but not before he led us to many of the compounds around the world where the opposition to the New World Order has set up their camps. "We befriended him, got his confidence and were able to track his movements. On the screen behind me, you will see the scope and size of this movement. All peoples refusing the mark are congregating in these places, Christians, Jews, Muslims, and all kinds of riff-raff rebels.

"We've been amassing our armed forces around these places. We are coordinating the start of this police action with the start of the sacrifices in the Temple. We want to send a message to anyone who thinks they can resist the mark of the Beast or his ultimate authority that their efforts will be futile and we will prevail!"

Mr. Baker strutted around for another half hour pounding on the podium, working the crowd into a frenzy until every last one of them was shouting for the blood of the rebels. When he sat down, he glanced at Mr. Rothfellas, who sat motionless with a gleam in his eyes. The bit-coin generated by this "police action" would put him again in total control of all the wealth in the world.

While the delegates were still frenzied, Chione instructed them to unanimously support the effort to bring to justice these rebels by pushing the yes tab on their vote pads. It didn't matter if there were any dissentions, when the vote was broadcast, and when the vote was presented to the Beast, it would be unanimous.

The rumblings of the war machine shook the earth as all prepared for battle.

26

Rag Tag Rebels

Joe Beason was the self-appointed leader of the refugees in the province of Colorado in the former USA. Nobody else wanted the responsibility. Their ranks were growing exponentially daily as the armies of the New World Order rolled through the towns and cities destroying everything in sight. The survivors ran searching for safety and some way to respond to the scorched earth policy of the Order.

Food and shelter were the top priority for now. Winters in his province were brutal and long. For now, the best strategy was to survive. The small bands scattered all over the territory foraged and hunted for food and pilfered anything not tied down from the New Order when they could.

Joe tried to organize some of the ex-military into a band of guerilla fighters and was having some luck, but they were armed with leftover ancient firearms that the former government missed during its last gun confiscation.

The rumors that weapons were available spread through the encampments, but the plans never materialized. The problem as he saw it was more lack of leadership than lack of supplies. At least for now, he and his counterparts could tweak the nose of this monster military they faced, but there was no goal, hope, or strategy.

Joe knew that if the resistance succeeded, they would need guidance. In his mind, there was only one man that could fill the void and keep them alive. He was Joe's captain in the marines, Montgomery Marshal.

Marshal was rumored to live in these mountains ever since his court martial. Montgomery Marshal was the greatest military strategist the marines had ever seen. He seemed to know the enemy's every move. While the other captains were rubbing elbows with their superiors at lavish parties designed to grease the wheels for promotion, he was studying the enemy. He disdained politics of any kind and that caused his downfall.

He was too efficient, too successful. When planning a mission, he used fewer resources and lost fewer men in battle than any other outfit in the latest desert war. The Pentagon hated when the armed services and the appropriations committees cited Captain Marshal's "success with less" policy, especially when the military asked for more funding. He refused the kickbacks and graft that was so common and accepted among all the other officers. They seemed to be getting rich off the suffering.

They set him up to fail. When his men got into battle, all support was pulled away. The drone strike to support his men's position didn't happen. The supply line vanished. The enemy overwhelmed their position and threatened to annihilate every one of his men, but his fierce loyalty to his men and his brilliant strategy pushed the enemy back long enough to allow his men to survive and inflict many enemy casualties as they escaped. They weren't called Devil Dogs for nothing.

Joe remembered the rush through enemy lines as if it was yesterday. While they were regrouping at the captain's designated rendezvous point, they heard the thunder in the background well after they were gone. They learned later that every civilian in their wake had been destroyed. The headlines and planted evidence indicated Captain Marshal was responsible for the carnage. Joe and the entire unit knew it wasn't the case, but the captain was tried and convicted.

In the end, the captain was court marshaled and given a dishonorable discharge. Joe left at the end of his tour along with everyone in his unit. He lost track of the captain, but rumor had it that he had a cabin in these mountains. Joe followed the rumors hoping his hunch was right.

He had been searching for weeks and was about to quit after many leads faded into folklore when he came across an old man named Marley. Mountain people called him Gnarly Marley. Joe thought he'd met a leprechaun when he first saw Marley. He walked with a cane that was as gnarled as he was. His eyes didn't look in the same direction at the same time, and his beard couldn't hide the wrinkles born of too much sun, and cold, and age. He held a pipe clenched in teeth almost the same color of his leathery skin. When he talked, he held his pipe in his free hand but clenched it again as soon as he finished talking.

When they met on the trail, the pipe came out and he spoke.

"What brings you up the mountain?" he said, eyeing Joe with suspicion.

"My name is Joe, and I'm looking for someone."

"If they's here shouldn't be too hard to find. Ain't many some ones up here."

"His name is Captain Montgomery Marshal. He was my captain in the marines. I need his help."

Marley was still sizing up this stranger like an old dog sniffing for danger. After what seemed a long time to Joe, he spoke, "There's only one I know in these parts besides me. Don't know his name 'cause nobody's brave enough to deliver his Welcome Wagon!"

Marley squinted at Joe for the least reaction to his sarcasm. Joe caught it. The corner of his mouth curled slightly. Marley decided he'd open up to this stranger.

"There's a fella lives on that ridge over there," Marley offered as he pointed with his cane to the location. "I only seen him once. I's tracking some game up the mountain one day and 'afore I knowed it, I was in his territory. I didn't think he know'd I was around. He was busy with an old grizzly.

"When they met on the trail, they's both surprised. That ole' grizzly reared up to his full height and filled the whole mountain with his growlin'. I figured the fella would turn tail and run. The bear did too. But he whipped out two bowie knives the size of machetes and did some growling of his own.

"Them knives was polished so bright they reflected the sun like a mirror. Every time the bear reared up, he'd turn them knives so they reflected right in the bear's eyes and blinded him with the flash. That ole bear rubbed his eyes like he's groomin', and 'bout the time his eyes focused, and he reared again. The Ole man would flash his knives again. The ole bear swiped his paws in the air to trin' to swat whatever wus getting' in his eyes."

"Purty soon that ole bear knew he was bested, so he turned tail and run! I swear Ole man didn't see me but he knew I was there. He turned my direction and grinned as he sheathed those knives and went right back about his business like nuthin' happened!"

Joe listened to the old timer's tale with a picture of Captain Marshal in his mind. The way Joe knew the captain made the yarn believable. That was just the kind of off the wall stuff he'd seen in the military. The enemy thought Captain Marshal was a demon or ghost.

Marley caught the faraway look in Joe's eyes. "I swear on my momma's grave I'm tellin' the truth. I saw it with my own eyes!"

"I believe you. I was just thinking about the captain and that's something I can see him doing."

"Don't get a chance to tell that story very often, but I think you's the first that didn't question the rant of an old man."

"They don't know the captain like I do!"

Joe waved at the old man and headed up the mountain. He knew he'd found his man. Marley watched Joe as he trekked up the mountain for a bit and moved on in his own quest for survival.

27

Captain Montgomery

Joe made his way up the mountain. He knew even if he found the captain, there was no guarantee he would help the cause. Still, he trekked on. He was breathing hard, and so he decided to stop for a few minutes. He slid his backpack off onto a rock and bent over with his hands on his knees. He couldn't remember ever getting this winded when he went on patrol back in the day, but that was in a desert and a long time ago. Now he was at the mercy of the altitude, and his age.

He finally straightened and stretched. Joe was about to reach for his pack when he felt the blade on his neck. He froze in place. He knew one small misunderstanding, and his blood would run down the trail he just walked up.

"What business you got on my mountain?" someone hissed in a familiar voice. Just the tone of his words used to strike fear in his men.

"It's me, Captain, lieutenant Joe Beason!"

The captain recognized the voice even after all these years, but the knife didn't move. "You couldn't be my lieutenant. None of my men would let the enemy get the drop on them like this." The captain could never miss an opportunity for a teaching moment, even now.

"Turn around slowly with your arms in the air!"

Joe felt the grip on his collar loosen so he complied. The first thing he saw was one of the Bowie knives Marley described gleaming in the light.

The knife posture changed just enough to let Joe know he wasn't going to die right now. Joe looked the man in the eye and reflexively made a saluting gesture.

"I'm not in military anymore, Lieutenant. Put that ridiculous hand down!" commanded Marshal.

Deep down, he appreciated the respect. He could be railroaded out of the marines, but no one could take the marine out of him.

"What are you doing on my mountain, Lieutenant?"

"Looking for you, sir." Joe replied.

Joe noticed the wrinkles around those eyes. A full grey beard hid the ravages of the harsh weather and time on the rest of Marshal's face, but Joe still felt the commanding presence.

"What, you want to reminisce about old times?" Marshal asked agitated.

"No, sir. I, along with thousands of refugees collecting in these mountains, need your help.

"Yeah, I've seen them. What concern is that of mine?"

"It's not going to stop, sir. They will keep coming until the government finds them. When the New World Order soldiers come, these hills are going to run red with the blood of these innocents. All they want is to be left alone, just like you. Their only crime is to not take the mark of the Beast so they can be tracked like animals and annihilated on a whim of the government."

Marshal didn't say anything so Joe continued, "You, of all people, are ought to know what happens when politics encroaches on decent people."

Marshal still didn't reply, but Joe saw in his eyes he was deep in thought.

"Besides, sir, you'll be overrun up here if we don't take back our lives."

Marshal felt the sun leaving over the mountain ridge to his west. He turned to face the sunset and drink in the calm. The serenity was the only thing that calmed his rage after he was court-martialed. The marines were his life. Part of him died that day. Now the solitude that he craved was threatened.

"Not my fight, Lieutenant," he said with his back still turned to Joe.

He started to walk away leaving Joe alone on the trail.

"I guess you're not the man I thought you were, Captain," Joe fired at him as he walked away.

Joe gathered his composure and his pack and started his long journey down the mountain. His thoughts turned to the survival of the refugees. The take-no-prisoners policy of the New World Order meant sure death. Still, for most refugees, it was better than the mark even as the only option.

Joe got to his four-wheeler for the final ride down the mountain and back home. He thought sure this is what God wanted him to do. He couldn't understand why Marshal didn't come on board. He tried his best. Maybe he should have gone with his wife and kids when they all saw the image on the silicon paper. At least he knew they were safe.

He missed them the most at night when he tried to sleep. Images flashed across his mind of all the good times. Funny, absence seemed to make all the times good times. The soldier inside wouldn't let him go. He didn't begrudge the ones that did. He just had to serve and protect.

He shrugged to himself and punched in the code for the four-wheeler to head back down the mountain. When he looked up, the captain was standing in his path.

"Got to thinking," he said. "I got a friend on the mountain that won't understand why all the commotion when they come for me. That old grizzly has been on this mountain way longer than me. We're both too old to start over.

"Bring me your recon. I've been doing some myself. I knew all about the troop movements. I just didn't know why."

The marshal disappeared into the landscape. Joe grinned from ear to ear while driving down the mountain.

The faith of a mustard seed, Joe thought to himself. He bowed his head and apologized to God for his little faith.

28

The Eagle's Nest

How am I going to get the information the captain will demand?

He thought of the folded silicon paper he always carried with him. It was his only link to his family. After returning to his base camp, he took it out of its pouch. He wasn't sure how it could help, but he felt led to open it. He didn't want to have to ask for forgiveness twice in one day for lack of faith.

As soon as his fingers touched the paper, he knew he had to get to the level clearing a few meters away from his position.

Joe walked into the command tent to find his second in command, Don Brennon. Don was a sergeant in the regular Army, retired, a fact that Joe brought up every chance he got for some good-natured ribbing.

"Don, I found Captain Marshal on a mountain a few klicks away!"

Don's eyes lit up. The man was legendary all branches of the military. When Joe went in search of his old boss, Don was skeptical about his chances of finding him but sometimes you got to do what you got to do. Especially when there are few options.

"Is he going to get involved?"

"Yes." Joe replied, "but now I have another problem. He needs recon. I could give him what little I have, but he already knows as must as I do. He needs to get inside their head and know what makes them tick."

"I'm going to go to the Eden. They have the technology to fly anywhere in this hostile environment they want without being detected. Maybe they could help gather the intel we need. I'm going to go plead with them to help. I don't feel I have any other option. I need you to continue to be in charge for a day or two while I'm away."

"Yes, Sir." Don replied, "good luck and God's speed."

That is what Joe was counting on.

He walked to the clearing carrying nothing but the paper. He didn't see the craft until the ramp lowered and the light from within beckoned him. He walked up the ramp and it immediately closed.

A middle-aged man was at the controls. Joe saw the Semper Fi tattooed on his massive arm and recognized him as a fellow marine.

The man thrust a huge right hand at Joe and he shook it. "Name's Jake Tanner."

"Joe Beason."

"I'll get you where you need to be, Joe. I know you are curious about the craft and how we got together, so I'll give you the answers that I can. The trip is a short hop out of these mountains, so I won't have your attention long.

Joe felt the heaviness of the acceleration as Jake expertly guided the craft and talked about their destination. In minutes, they were hovering over a lush garden in preparation to land.

Mary was elated when Elias' son James shared the news about Joe's return. She worried about him constantly. His path in life was a difficult one for them, but she knew that men with the passion, compassion, and sense of duty like her Joe had to heed the call when there was a need for protection and service.

When Joe stepped off the ramp, his wife and kids were waiting. The two children were jumping up and down in anticipation of seeing their daddy. His wife rushed to him and jumped into his arms, smothering him with wet teary kisses before she found his lips, trying her best to become as one. Joe swung her around as the tears welled. The children each grabbed a leg and held on for dear life to make sure he couldn't leave again. They all talked at once vying for his attention. Jake looked at them with a smile. He remembered his service and the fact that he did this work for his children.

"Follow me," Jake said after the family reunion.

Joe scooped up his two kids and followed with his wife, Mary, clinging to his arm. The fragrances of the garden filled his head. He felt at ease, content in the moment. Jake led him to the dining area so the family could enjoy a meal together before they settled in.

Jake went to find Elias, his good friend and the head of the council of this Eden. From the information Joe gave, Jake knew Elias should be informed.

"How's it going, Elias?"

Elias' face lit when he recognized his old friend. Although they were in the same compound, their paths seldom crossed. Elias was busy with affairs of the state, and Jake flew an Eagle from here to there, wherever the bit-chain algorithms and God led.

They locked right thumbs in the man-shake and went in for the man hug.

"How are things going in the Eagle?" he asked.

"Great!" Jake replied. "Best job I ever had. I really feel like I'm making a difference in the world for a change."

"Believe me, brother, you are! So, what brings you down to earth?" Elias replied.

"I brought in a fella by the name of Joe today. His family was already here. He tells me that vast armies are gathering to annihilate any group that refuses the mark. He could use our help."

"Yes, I'm aware of his arrival. I've been very troubled by the reports. Those people will be slaughtered if we don't help. Even if they don't see the image, there is still hope for those who refuse take the mark. When he gets settled, why don't you bring him by and we'll hear what he has to say."

Joe and Mary strolled through the compound hand in hand with the kids bouncing around them. She leaned her head on his arm as they walked. It had been months since she last saw Joe. There was very little opportunity to communicate because the Eagles were the only thing that could breach the dimension between her world and his. God's security was perfect.

Joe basked in the radiant light that seemed to come from every direction at once. It was as bright as the sun, but it didn't burn his skin. He felt peace like never before. He knew it was because of the light.

A group of children were playing in the lush grass in a meadow beside the path. Little Joey and his sister Pam looked at their mother for permission to go to them. She nodded, and they were off as fast as they could run.

Joe caught the interaction, and it cut him deeply. Since he was gone so much, the children naturally looked to their mother for guidance. He missed so much of their lives in his absence. His "maybe somedays" were racing by with every missed birthday.

Jake caught up with the couple and asked Joe if he could meet with Elias and him after the next sleep cycle. Joe was puzzled why they called night a sleep cycle.

"Sure, I'll be there."

"Okay, Joe. I'll see you after breakfast tomorrow."

Jake waved in an almost salute and left the family to get re-acquainted.

When fatigue overtook Joe, Mary gathered the kids and they headed for their home in the mountain. Mary placed her hand on the door palm first. It swung open for the children. Joe followed her in.

He'd never been in the house but felt at home instantly. The kids each had their own room, and there was a spacious master bedroom and a pristine bath but he noted that there was no kitchen. *I guess no one needs a kitchen with this bounty of food and the volunteers to cook it,* he thought.

The only good thing about being apart is the feeling of being like newlyweds when we're together, he mused. They fell asleep still locked in each other's arms, bathed in the soothing light. Joe had never been so content.

The sleep cycle ended too soon for Mary. She knew he would be gone again soon. She caressed his cheek and he awoke to his dream. He drank in all that God had provided him.

A knock on the door intruded on their bliss. They gathered the kids and walked in the garden to a morning meal, still locked at the heart. Joe felt duty intruding on his life once again even as they ate.

Elias and Jake entered the room and settled in for a meal. Joe recognized the banter of old friends. When he was finished with his meal, they motioned him over to their table.

"Joe, tell us how we could best help you and the cause," Elias urged.

"We are outgunned, outmanned, and by earthly logic, should throw up our hands to the mercy of the New World Order," Joes said. "Except they have no mercy, and we will be exterminated on the whim of the Beast and his people. I've talked with one of the best military minds in the world about helping us and he has agreed, but he needs intelligence reports. We're not asking you to fight. We'll do that part. I'm not sure why I'm here but I felt led to come here and ask for help."

"Elias and I have been talking. The craft that brought you here, the Eagle, has the best cloaking device in the world. We've snatched people from the middle of a crowded park and no one knew," Jake interjected.

"Julie, the inventor of the system, and her team are constantly upgrading it, and so far, no one has been able to detect us, "Elias said. "If you can supply us with the New World Order's known positions, we can use the Eagles to scout them for you.

"Although they weren't designed as spy planes, I think they would be ideally suited for that purpose with just a few modifications like the addition of state-of-the-art cameras. Since Jake and I are familiar with the craft, we will be the ones to try out the new calling for the Eagles. You stay behind and enjoy your family."

Elias knew from his past what it was like to be separated from family. "It will take our team a cycle to install the new system so we'll be on our way after two sleep cycles. When we have evaluated the Eagle's usefulness, we'll get back to you."

Joe was gratcful for the time with his family. He was having second thoughts about ever leaving. He'd never experienced this kind of peace.

29

Radical Recon

Elias was writing the software for the new spy system while the cameras were mounted under the belly of the two Eagles, just under the ramp. The three-hundred sixty-degree lens simplified the mechanics of the setup. The software could pick up the information and project a three-dimensional image of everything it detected. If the Eagles could keep from being detected, the rebels would have at their disposal the greatest intelligence gathering system ever built.

The sleep cycles came and went. The preliminary tests looked flawless. It was time to go into the field and run the real-time data collection. Elias had been dreading his next move. He had to tell his wife, Abby, he would be going back into the field. The last time he left was disastrous. He almost died in that Dubai high-rise underestimating the power of the

Trilateral technology. Without God's intervention, his reliance on technology would have been fatal.

Abby rose from the sleep cycle to find Elias already out. Not unusual for him. When he was puzzled, he walked in the garden. The peace and solitude allowed him to commune with his Creator.

She met him walking back to their home. They naturally ended up in each other's arms for their good-morning kiss. They started the wake cycle this way always. They sought out one another before their service to the people started and embraced, kissed, and prayed. She knew before he said anything that he was troubled.

"Abby, I need you to take over for me. I've been called to go into the field and do some testing with the Eagle. We have installed new software and cameras in an experiment to help those left behind."

She pulled away and cringed. The last time he left her he almost failed to return. Yet she knew he would do what he was led to do.

"Matthew 18:12. 'How think ye? If a man have a hundred sheep and then one be gone astray doth he not leave the ninety-nine and goeth into the mountains and seeketh the one which is gone astray?'" He quoted with much flair and pomp, trying to get his point across.

He always used the King James Version of the Bible when he wanted to be dramatic with his delivery and make a point. There were probably a few left behind, and they needed a chance for the protection God had supplied them.

"I don't know if it will make a difference, but we have to try," Elias said. "God expects no less than our best effort. We have been given the mandate to save all of the believers. If we've missed only one, that is one too many."

"Of course I will take over," she replied, missing him already. "How long will you be gone?"

"Not long. We will test the Eagles and gather what data we need. If all goes   right, we can turn the operation over to Joe so he can coordinate the worldwide mission to save the lost."

He hadn't been out of Eden since he first arrived at this location. He was apprehensive and excited that God had put on his heart to go after the lost. Excited to be in the field but apprehensive about leaving Abby and his family. He shouldn't be, after seeing how God multiplied their meager mountain into the paradise it was today, but his human nature was limiting his faith again.

"I think we shouldn't be gone more than five of our sleep cycles," he said. "I don't know any more what that translates into in earth time. Because of the nature of our mission, we won't have any communication with you until we return. I have some last-minute details to attend to. Then Jake and I will be on our way. I'll say goodbye to the kids before I leave." With that, he walked away, blowing her a kiss as he did.

She was comforted that Jake would be part of the mission. He helped Elias when he was a fugitive on the run after his family was killed. God had put them together then and she could only pray that the outcome would be the same this time.

Deep in thought, he walked to the compound where others were performing last-minute checks on the two Eagles that were retro-fitted for the spy mission. The last project with Marcus and DAN didn't turn out as planned. Marcus lost his life and DAN was destroyed, but the Beast survived.

I know Revelations says the Beast survived a fatal blow and was healed, but that doesn't make the fact that my friend Marcus lost his life and our technology failed any easier to swallow.

He was still struggling with his lack of faith and self-doubts when he entered the place where the Eagles took flight. His spirit lifted as he saw the technicians readying the crafts. They were majestic, just like their namesake. He always admired these great birds and their ability to bridge the gap between the world and these Edens on a minute's notice. Elias spotted his best friend and mentor Darious, who personally supervised the conversion of his creation into the new version. He believed God brought him and Elias together at the right time, under the right circumstances, to create these marvels.

"I think they're ready," Darious said, beaming. "We will brief you and Jake on the operation of the cameras and you can be on your way."

He was very proud of what he and Elias had accomplished with God's guidance. These Eagles were playing an important part in keeping all Christians safe in these perilous end times.

"Sounds good! I need to say goodbye to the kids and Abby and I'll be ready." Jake walked toward his family also to say goodbye as they were finishing the conversation.

"We'll brief you in the conference room before you leave." Darious said.

Jake and Elias nodded and walked away, letting Darious finish his business.

This was routine for Jake, but Elias hadn't flown since they established this colony and other priorities took over. He couldn't contain his exuberance. He knew other pilots were more qualified, but he developed the three--dimensional cameras and wrote the software so he was the best choice for troubleshooting the new system. He chatted away as they walked.

Jake just nodded and grinned. He thought back to when they met. He still slipped once in a while and called Elias David. David was running from the people that murdered his family so he changed his identity from David Alonzo Browning, the billionaire teenager, to Elias Tobias, the computer tech. Jake knew him as David when he stowed away between two large culverts Jake was hauling in his truck. They got off to a rocky start, but the kid helped him grieve the loss of his own son and in the process, they grew close.

They became partners in crime when Elias enlisted his help to truck then experimental Eagles to Area Fifty-One, so they could test the machines in the dark phase of the moon in the middle of the night. Because the Eagles didn't have sophisticated cloaking capabilities at that time, and their tear-drop shape, they could easily be mistaken for alien space craft.

It was on that mission that Jake got his first ride in an Eagle. He knew from that first encounter that he would someday pilot one. Never in his wildest dreams did he think of the impact he would have in saving so many of God's children.

Elias was still chatting away when they came to his house. Jake didn't say a word. Elias walked on and didn't stop until Jake shoved his shoulder.

"Little excited, are we? Jake chided.

Elias blushed. "Yeah, just a little."

He went in to find Duane, James, Arlane, and Abby waiting. He hugged each one and briefed Abby on what was going to happen. They chatted about everyday things. Abby asked questions she already knew the answers to just to hear him talk. Her anxiety mingled with his excitement. It was real in this room. All he truly lived for was now in his arms. He felt guilty for being so excited to leave.

Time raced by as it always does when families have to say goodbye. Elias hugged them all hard, trying to squeeze out the last bit of love he would miss in the coming cycles. It wasn't going to be a long separation, but any separation in these uncertain times was trying. He walked out stifling tears and proceeded to the briefing.

Jake caught up with him, and they walked side by side almost in military step. Jake noticed Elias' subdued demeanor where excitement ruled just moments ago.

"Goodbyes are tough, eh kid?" Jake remarked.

Elias made a brief eye contact to confirm what Jake said. Jake was ex-military and drove a truck before piloting the Eagle. Goodbyes were as much a part of life to his family as breathing. Still after all his farewells, he felt the anxious tug.

They walked into the briefing room in silence. The din of the small gathering brought them back to their senses, letting them know the time for action was now. Personal feelings faded, replaced by the unity of purpose a common mission creates. Elias and Jake took their seats, and Darious began immediately.

"People, we are faced with a crisis that defines the future of the refugees the New World Order has targeted for disposal. I know that most of these people are not Christians, but they are children of God just as we are, and our Christian mandate is to give them every chance possible to get right with God. To that end, I want Elias to lead off with the characteristics of his cameras and what we can expect, followed by

Julie who will explain the updates in the cloaking system."

Elias talked for a short while. The holographic images wouldn't be broadcast over the communication system for fear of detection. All the data would be analyzed on their return. Joe would be involved in that process to determine what data his captain would require.

Julie briefed them on some of the improvements the cloaking system had undergone. It was now possible to project images on the hull of the ship at the speed of sound and slightly beyond. The range and speed of the craft were greatly enhanced. The hum of the energy generators could be heard before the craft could be seen. Her recommendation was to keep a minimum range of one kilometer from their target.

The cameras can see the dirt under their fingernails at that range! Elias smiled to himself.

Darious stood and prayed before dismissing the group. Everyone in the room wished the pilots Godspeed as the two walked toward the launch area.

"I'm the lead, and you're the wing on this mission, Elias," Jake said. "I can get out of this place with my eyes closed. Just do as I do and we'll be fine."

Elias nodded. It would take him a little while to get his wings on again. He was grateful for his friend's confidence. A familiar swoosh let the boarding ramp down, and Elias disappeared into the belly of the craft. Old memories of past missions flooded his brain. If it hadn't been for these crafts, he would have perished in Dubai. That seemed a long time ago now. He didn't have time now to go down memory lane. His focus shifted to his pre-flight protocol.

The hum of the craft changed pitch, and he knew he was ready. He signaled Jake and they hovered for an instant and disappeared from sight as the cloaking device engaged. He locked his sonar onto Jake's craft and followed him into the other world. After leaving Eden, he glanced down on the monitor and the garden had disappeared. The landscape seemed undisturbed, as if Eden didn't exist.

While Elias was pondering over that fact, his sonar blared, warning him that Jake's Eagle was already traveling near the speed of sound and was in danger of getting out of tracking range. Elias rolled the control and sank into his seat almost helpless from the g-force. He was rusty. He needed to keep his focus on the matter at hand.

Jake decelerated as quickly as he accelerated and settled in on Joe's Mountain. Elias closed in fast and whipped by him like the tail on a dragon. He settled into position and vowed to pay close attention.

Jake smiled at the antics of his rusty wingman. Maybe he was showboating a little, but he knew Elias was a quick study. He focused on the task at hand. He slowed to the optimum speed agreed on at the briefing. They went about mapping the New World Order forces on Joe's Mountain and settled on the coordinates Joe supplied. They would follow the supply chain to its source and track the troop movements back to the largest base they could find.

The days turned into tedious routine. They mapped as much as they could before settling in on a hidden part of the mountain. They ate rations they brought and slept in the machine, never shutting down power, ready to flee at a moment's notice. Sometimes they lowered the ramp and walked out into the brisk mountain air to find a clear pool of pure mountain water and just to revive and stretch their muscles.

Days turned into a week and a week into two. The cameras recorded everything that happened on the mountain. Finally, it was time to return to base and analyze their newfound knowledge. They were both ready to get home.

Elias was ready for Jake's burst of speed this time and stayed with him. In a few short minutes, they were descending back into their Eden.

Joe, Darious, and the technicians needed to download and process the data as soon as possible, so they met Jake and Elias when they landed. Homecoming would have to wait.

Joe sat at a computer station with a joystick in his right hand, dumbfounded as the middle of the room came to life. The technician showed him how to zoom in and out with his left hand. A grid overlay showed him exactly where he was on the map. He zoomed in on a random soldier guarding a refrigerated truck with Amy's logo on the side. He could see the color of the guard's eyes.

He played with the controls and asked the technicians question after question until he was familiar with the setup.

The captain is going to love this! He thought. *He will pore over this for hours until he knows every movement of the NWO soldiers. He'll know their movements better than the NWO commanders.*

"When can we take this to Captain Marshal?" Joe inquired.

"We are prepared to get it to him after the next sleep cycle. Right now, Jake and I just want to clean up and reconnect with our families."

"You got that right, buddy. I need to clean off this mountain grime and rest my weary bones!"

"Elias, I'll take Joe and this intel to Captain Marshall after the next sleep cycle. You've got an empire to run. Let the marines do what we do best!"

"Okay."

Elias didn't put up a fight. This mission reminded him of the last time he was in an Eagle and the near-death experience in Dubai that humbled him into submission to God. He knew to leave the mission in their capable hands.

30

Clandestine Hope

Captain Marshall was going about his morning routine on the mountain when he heard a voice behind him. He whirled around, his handgun drawn in one hand and a gleaming blade in another. Joe swore the captain had his teeth bared like a cornered badger.

"Good morning, sir!" Joe was enjoying the fact that he got the drop on his former superior. He grinned from ear to ear and raised his hand in salute.

"How many times do I have to tell you, lieutenant, don't salute me?"

"Yea, sir!" Joe put his hand down after the captain returned his salute.

"What do you want this time?"

"I've got the recon you requested, and there is someone here I'd like you to meet."

Jake walked down the ramp of the Eagle and approached the two. He was carrying a backpack.

Sergeant Jake Tanner, I'd like you to meet Captain Montgomery Marshal." Jake's hand automatically went up in salute.

"I'm no longer a captain!" Marshal growled at Joe.

"Once a marine always a marine, sir!" Jake snapped and brought his hand down.

The captain shook his head in resignation.

"We have something for you." Jake removed a device that looked like a virtual gamers' helmet. "If you wear this headset with this control, you can access all the data we gathered in the last two weeks. It contains troop movements, troop strength, armament strength, and anything else you need to know about the NWO forces threatening Joe's people and your mountain."

The captain hesitated for a minute, weighing the threat against the benefit, as he always did before acting. He decided that it was time to let people, especially people like Joe and Jake, back into his life.

"Come with me," he said, walking away.

Jake put the helmet back in its place. Joe and Jake looked at each other and followed. A few meters down a barely passable trail, the captain disappeared into a crevice in the rock forming the side of the mountain. They followed, turning sideways in one place to get past.

The passage opened into a natural cavern formed when the mountain was born. Tons of rock covered the captain's lair. The spacious room was neat and orderly, reflecting its current occupant. Light came from solar powered lamps and natural ventilation came from somewhere deep in the mountain. It kept the space at sixty-two degrees all year round. The snowmelt supplied all the water the captain needed.

Joe and Jake marveled at his man cave. No one would ever suspect that something this elaborate would exist in this hard-to-reach side of a mountain. The captain preferred it this way. Joe was dying of military curiosity. He knew the captain had an arsenal somewhere in the mountain but decided now was not the time to ask about it.

When their awe subsided, Jake opened his backpack and produced the helmet.

"Put this on, and I'll walk you through the controls," Jake said. "We can show you anything you need to know about the enemy. A grid will appear first, then the geographic layout, then the bases involved in this area. Supply lines, troops, weapon caches, type of weapons, anything you need to know. If you so desire, sir, I can show you the bathroom habits of their commanding officer."

The captain put on the device.

"If you take this control, you can zoom in on a target or zoom out on a landscape," Jake continued. "Also, if you want to record details, there is an audio button you can use to record notes as you go and an editing button so you can edit any part of the information."

The captain was ready for this new challenge "I've never seen detail and scope like this," he said. "How did you get this in such a short time?"

"Can't tell you that, Captain," Jake replied. "But we have the capability to go anywhere undetected at a minute's notice. We're dead serious about stopping this massacre and many more that are about to take place all over the world."

"Hmmm," the captain grunted.

He was engrossed in his newfound knowledge. The more comfortable he got with the technology, the more questions he had.

"What are these trucks with the "A" emblem on the side?" he asked. "It seems like they put a lot of manpower in protecting them. They don't have that many guards on their weapons and their security."

"That is the amygdaloideum. It is the weapon the Beast used to gain control of the world. Once you have ingested it, it will kill you, make you deathly sick, or make you its slave. So far, no one has an answer to its devastation."

"Hmmm, duly noted," the captain said.

"I've got to get back to my people, and Jake has to get back to his commitments," Joe declared.

"I'll see you in a week. I'll show at eighteen-hundred hours in your compound with my findings. We'll formulate our plan of action then. I'll need to know your stats at that time."

Joe was encouraged by the captain's tone. He had things to do in preparation.

Jake, can you drop me in the compound?" he asked. "Here are the coordinates."

"Sure."

Joe and Jake found their own way back to the Eagle. The technology and all its data were left in the capable hands of the captain.

Joe rode in silence. He was already missing his family. He was getting too old to save the world. His body and mind reeled against the harsh conditions in the camp. He was overwhelmed with the needs of so many. He was not above sending raiding parties to known NWO strongholds and pilfering supplies.

"They need so much," Joe said almost to himself.

Jake sensed his agony. "What kind of stuff do you need?"

Joe replied almost absently, caught in his own agony, not realizing that the Great Provider was listening in the form of Jake Tanner.

"Food mainly. These mountains are going to get very unforgiving in a few months. It's hard to fight right on an empty stomach. And shelter. These tents are going to get cold. And medicines, and doctors, and medics."

"Jake, I'm scared. I can't do this alone."

"Joe! Joe! Joe! You're not alone! Gods got your back!" Jake lectured sternly. "He's got this!"

"Yeah, I know, but sometimes it gets intense!"

Joe put his marine face on and hit the ground running.

31

The Calvary Arrives

J ake sought out Elias when he got back.

"We need to talk, buddy." Jake's heart was still heavy. He hated leaving the marine behind without doing something.

"Sure. What's up?"

"When I took Joe back, he almost broke down. The burden he's under would crush a lesser man."

"Yeah, I agree. He's looking down the throat of the Beast whose mouth is opened wide."

"What if we took them supplies? Is that something God would approve of? We have so much in here and they have so little out there."

"I know we don't need to bring anything in with us and we can't contaminate the Edens with unbelievers, but what about taking things out?"

Elias thought for a short minute.

"I'm all for it, but you know I'm not really in charge here. God is. Let's ask him!"

Everyone in Eden was informed and asked to pray. They all knew that finding any Christians in the world was a long shot, but they also knew they had to try.

God answered. The outpouring of faith was overwhelming. Many people volunteered to help. Doctors and nurses volunteered to go back into the world. Some gathered food and clothing, some volunteered to be missionaries to the lost souls, and some helped by praying.

Jake's flights to retrieve the children of God had dwindled in the last months as last of the faithful came into the fold. This came at the right time. The Eagles now were commissioned to feed the lost.

He felt rejuvenated. He felt like that young marine he used to be. He had all of the available Eagles in the fleet at his disposal. One after one was loaded full and sent to Joe's Mountain.

Jake led the first craft. He wanted to see the look on Joe's face when the supply line got in full gear.

The volunteers started unloading the supplies in the dark of night. All the security people had been forewarned so no one would get shot. Joe was floored. He knew all about Edens, but he didn't realize the scope of God' love for the lost. He hoped more would be brought to Christ through these selfless acts.

"The marines have landed, so to speak," Jake said, smiling to Joe when they finally met.

Joe could only grab his hand in a man-shake and go in for a man-hug. He was speechless and on the verge of tears.

"Gotta go get loaded again, see ya on the flip flop." The trucker in Jake snuck out.

For the next two nights, the Eagles kept landing full and taking off empty. Jake hoped that soon he would return to Eden with passengers.

32

Military Planning

True to his word, Captain Montgomery walked into the camp a week later at eighteen-hundred hours. Joe was ready. He convened a meeting of all the leaders in the rebel forces.

When the captain came in the room, chairs shuffled as they all stood at attention.

"At ease, ladies and gentlemen," he said. "I've been asked to evaluate the strategies of this outfit in regards to an upcoming conflict.

"Frankly, you don't have a chance, but neither did Americans during the revolution against the British Empire, the most powerful nation on the earth at that time. Freedom and self-preservation are powerful motivators. Now you are fighting for your freedom, and your lives.

"Why were the British defeated? I'll answer my own question.

1. They were fighting on our turf.

2.   They were controlled by a central chain of command that couldn't react to battlefield situations.

3.   They fought their style of war and were too rigid to change.

4. Their supply lines were vulnerable.

"The rebels struck and disappeared into the landscape. Guerrilla warfare. The British couldn't find them. When the British command heard of this, they didn't, or couldn't regroup. They continued to be sitting ducks. The guerrilla style warfare ambushed their supply lines by sinking their ships in our harbors, and striking the supply wagons before they could reach the troops. We have to exploit this enemy's weakness if we are going to survive this ordeal."

Captain Montgomery Marshal had a way of rallying his troops. They were spellbound by his presence. Lieutenant Joe knew this was his greatest asset and their only hope.

"Our armament, compared to theirs, is like throwing sticks and stones at a brick wall," the captain continued. "We must, must, exploit their weakness. In this case, it is the dependence on this Amy. If we can disrupt the shipments, the supply, of Amy for just a few hours, this mighty elite NWO army will self-destruct.

"I have supplied the what and why, and now we need to know the how. The main focus of NWO is the next shipment of this magic elixir. They put more emphasis on this than on their weapons, so this is not going to be an easy task. I'm opening this meeting to anyone who has any ideas on the subject."

The captain sat down and looked around the table for input. The room was a den of conversation, but no one spoke up. Joe sat passively, hoping for some miracle plan to emerge from all the noise. His mind wondered back to his family in Eden.

How he longed to be with them! He thought of Jake and Elias, and all the people who stepped in to help, giving up their own safety and comfort for this long shot. He thought about the first time he met Jake on his trip to Eden. Jake once said he used to be a trucker before he piloted his Eagle. Maybe he could help with some insight on how best to disable a truck load of poison.

"I gotta go. I'll be back as soon as I can," Joe whispered in the captain's ear.

The captain nodded. Joe disappeared out of the room.

I wonder if Jake has made his delivery today, Joe thought.

He walked quickly to the landing area to talk to the supply sergeant.

"Has Jake Tanner been here yet?" he asked.

"No, sir. He usually arrives around twenty-one hundred hours."

"Jake glanced at his watch. It was close to nineteen-hundred. "Don't let him leave without seeing me."

"Yes, sir."

Joe went back to the meeting to see if they made any progress. He listened to the proposals, but most consisted of direct military action or roadside bombs, or aerial assault, nothing the rebel forces had the manpower or resources to sustain.

The meeting disbanded with the agreement to meet the following day at the same time. They all needed the night to research the most feasible ideas.

Joe met with the supply clerks to get an updated inventory of the goods the Eagles had delivered to date. He was mulling over the latest figures when Jake walked in the door.

He saluted Joe, and Joe did the same. He began to understand the captain's reluctance to keep the military hierarchy alive by saluting. Jake was many years his senior, and there was no uniform, or stripes, or commissions involved. There was only a common enemy and a common goal.

"Supply clerk said you wanted to see me," Jake said.

Joe rose to his feet and shook Jake's hand. He just couldn't thank Jake enough for what he had put in motion to save the refugees. Now he had to ask him to help even more.

"Jake, you told me when you picked me up to go to Eden that you used to be a truck driver. I need to pick your brain about how to best disable and destroy a big rig, one that is heavily guarded and carrying the key to our survival. Any thoughts?"

Why would you want to destroy a perfectly good truck? Jake thought. All trucks were special to him. Sure, he had to destroy his share in the desert wars, but even that pained him.

Joe launched into a lengthy explanation on how Amy was the key to the rebel forces having a chance against the NWO armies and how the trucks were heavily guarded from the time they were loaded.

"Do the trucks have drivers?" Jake interrupted.

"No, they have the newest satellite-controlled technology. Why do you ask?"

Jake had a faraway look on his face and a grin that kept getting bigger. Joe quit his explanation mid-sentence.

"I once delivered a clandestine cargo to Area 51 in a truck I actually drove. Elias sat beside me all the way with a laptop. He got us through the electronic border checks and disabled the security on the base. We went right in like we owned the place!"

Joe had a marine Let's get-err-done smile., "Do you think he could disable the satellite feed to the trucks?"

"I'd bet my life on it, and yours too, for good measure!" Jake said.

"If I leave right now, I might be able to get back tomorrow with the plan in hand. The kid's that good!"

"Then go! I'll expect you back here at eighteen-hundred tomorrow."

There were no salutes now. They were two school boys linked by the greatest secret plan to prank the principal that had ever been devised.

Jake trotted back to his Eagle. He couldn't wait to tell Elias.

Elias sat at his computer station doing the mundane task of data entry, a necessary job, but one he loathed. Jake danced into the room and skipped around his desk, his excitement and adrenalin still pumping.

Elias grinned at this old man acting like his boys. "What's got into you?"

"I want to tweak the nose of a big ole Grizzly bear and live to tell about it, and I need your help."

Elias was amused and intrigued.

"Joe and I are fixen' to take on a hibernating Grizzly. Captain Marshall seems to think the Achilles' heel of the NWO forces is the dependence on Amy."

" Almost all, if not all of them are addicted to it and need a daily fix. They can't stockpile more than a week's supply before it loses some of its potency. If we can disrupt that supply, they will be more of a momma bear's cub that a mean ole full grown grizzly."

Elias felt intrigued. "How can I help?" he asked.

"Remember when we first tested the Eagles and I drove the truck from Detroit to Area 51 and back?"

"Yeah, I remember," Elias said with a grin. "That was a good time."

"These trucks are state of the art satellite controlled driverless vehicles. There is no safety backup embedded in the roads this far off the highways. We need a computer genius to hack the satellite feed so that we can control the guidance system in these trucks. Piece of cake for someone of your abilities, eh?"

Elias didn't answer right away. He was already churning out the program in his mind. He had the hardware from the Detroit trip so he could modify his software and hack the satellite feed.

"Piece of cake, Jake!"

Jake knew when someone mocked him.

"Did I mention that I need the system for my next load out tomorrow?"

"No, but I figured as much. You go get your beauty sleep. God knows you need it. I'll be up all night!"

Jake mimicked a violin player and laughed all the way out the door.

Elias went to warn Abby that he probably wouldn't make it to bed tonight. He was almost floating, as he felt the adrenalin flowing. He was happiest when he had a challenging task.

Elias walked in the garden in prayer. With a clear focus, he felt like an athlete limbering up for the big game; only his preparation was spiritual and mental.

Finally, he felt balanced and ready. He headed for his computer lab.

In the back of his filing cabinet, he found the laptop he used for the excursion across the country to test the Eagles. He marveled to himself how far the technology had advanced in such a short time. The Eagles now were nearly invisible and had much more capacity and speed than the old models. Once again, they would prove indispensable in protecting the faithful.

He copied the software and began his modifications. He fashioned a transponder that would pick out the right frequency the trucks used and a jamming circuit that enabled the computer to override the satellite and take control. An old-fashioned gamer control allowed the operator to drive the truck from anywhere within a two-kilometer radius.

He worked into the night, his fingers caressing the keys while his mind envisioned his creation. By morning, he was ready for the installation. He gathered his night's work and headed to Jake's Eagle. The technicians began the installation under his watchful eye. Jake sauntered in fully rested, sucking on a toothpick and reminiscing about his wonderful breakfast.

"Your Highness! Greetings from all your peons and slaves!" Elias bowed low, mocking him.

"Ahhh, ain't life grand!" Jake swooned, patting his belly. "You may rise and kiss my ring. You got my bird ready hot shot?"

"Of course, I have," Elias said. "I'll need to reteach the elderly pilot of this beautiful piece of machinery how to drive a truck again."

"Like riding a bike, Jake said. "Once you learn you got it for life."

"Yeah, but you've never done it from two klicks away and a thousand meters above it."

Elias shook his head at Jake's feigned arrogance. The technicians didn't quite know how to take the banter. They were a serious lot anyway. The tech gave Elias a nod that it was ready, so he placed his hand on the bird and lowered the ramp. Jake followed him in.

They did the preflight check as the bird hovered like an eagle over a wind shear on the side of a mountain. At Jake's commanding touch, it took flight.

They prowled the nearest highway looking for a single truck to test the system. It didn't take long to single out the prey. A lone truck headed west on a flat stretch of highway. Jake put the bird on automatic pilot while Elias booted up the equipment. The screen came alive with a real-time holograph of the truck and its surroundings. Jake took control. He could see the same thing a driver would see if there was one. He moved the controller, and the truck wobbled back and forth, tires squealing, almost out of control. Jake quickly corrected the input and the truck righted itself.

"Whoa there, cowboy!" Elias chimed. "Like riding a bike, eh?"

"Shut up!" Jake didn't take his eyes off the screen.

Elias burst out laughing. Jake stuck out tongue out the side of his mouth and rocked to the motion of the truck he was trying to control.

After a few minutes, Jake got full control of the truck and was getting comfortable with the quickness of his controller. He brought the truck to a stop in a truck stop and guided it back onto the highway.

"Nice job, Jake."

Jake glanced at Elias to see if he was being sarcastic or really meant what he said. Elias was sincere.

"Time for David to go slay Goliath," Jake said.

They headed back to Eden.

"This is where I get off," Elias said when they landed.

"He reached out in a man-shake. Be careful out there, Dad. I mean Jake."

He looked up at the hulk of a man with a sheepish grin.

Freudian slip, he wondered. Maybe in his exhausted state, old memories came back. He squelched them long ago in Albuquerque shortly after his dad was killed.

Jake found the sky and Elias rest. Elias prayed for Jake's safety before he dozed off.

33

The Secret Weapon

Jake landed in the refugee supply area with fifteen minutes to spare. He couldn't help a little saunter in his step as he walked into the meeting.

"I didn't think you were going to show," Joe said, relieved to see him.

"Sorry for not being here in time to brief you on the plan."

The gleam in his eye told Joe everything was good.

"Elias came through. We tested it on a civilian truck and it works fine. I can't wait to go after the Amy shipment if I get the chance. It's all up to you and the captain. Let me go last so I can explain the plan."

"Agreed."

They sat through the military solutions, all detailed and feasible. One group wanted to ambush while rounding the last switchback in the mountain before the NWO encampment. Another wanted to use guided missiles, another, roadside bombs.

"Jake, you're up!" Joe informed.

"All the plans I've heard here tonight are viable for a well-equipped militia, which we're not," Jake said. "I have a very unorthodox plan that will cost the movement nothing in military assets, and, if done right, no loss of lives on either side. I have a method of jamming the satellite transmissions that control the trucks on the road. In thirty seconds, I can drive any truck where I want from two kilometers away and one thousand meters in the air.

"Our intel tells us when the shipments come through. In one week, I can single handedly bring this NWO unit to its knees. No brag, just facts."

"What support do you need from us, Sergeant?" the captain asked.

"We'll need a raiding party about forty-eight hours after the shipment is sabotaged," Jake replied. "We need to assess the effect it is having on the troops. If our calculations are correct on the amount of Amy they have in reserve, we should be able to assess the effectiveness in that two-day period.

"Since this is a new operation, we will have to adjust our tactics as we go. I'm ready to strike the next shipment as soon as I'm authorized to do so."

The captain looked around the room for reaction and did what captains have to do. He led. "As far as I know, the next shipment is due at o-four hundred tomorrow morning. We will put together a team of volunteers with some of our best weapons and start toward the enemy lines. We'll coordinate with you after the truck is destroyed.

"I'll stick around to see if a replacement truck is deployed right away, in case I have to go after it as well. I hope they don't send drones or supply choppers in too soon. They will be a lot harder to deal with. We'll deal with that as we go," said Jake.

"Good hunting, Sergeant," replied the captain.

With that, the captain saluted Jake who saluted back. They were two old marines with the fire rekindled in their bellies.

Jake and Joe walked out of the meeting in silence. The old butterflies were building in Jake's stomach, the ones that heighten a man's awareness and survival instincts. Some might call it fear, some courage, but only a combat vet understands and channels the feeling.

When they arrived at the supply area, Jake patted the belly of the bird and the ramp lowered.

"Godspeed, my friend!"

Jake nodded and disappeared up the ramp. Joe stood his ground until the ramp raised and the Eagle started its liftoff. The disturbance in the energy fields around the Eagle caused the hair on his neck stand at attention and a sense of well-being flood his body.

He turned and double-timed back to the captain. He would lead the first team in the conflict.

Jake was on the hunt. Just like his craft's namesake, he soared through the heavens undetected by his prey. An hour later, he spotted a military convoy so he went in to investigate. Confirmed! His demeanor changed. He was now a big cat patiently stalking its prey. He aligned his bird with the convoy and followed at their speed. He had the advantage of seeing the landscape. He knew where the unpredictable mountain was going before the convoy did. He picked his spot.

The road entered a steep downhill grade before rounding a bend and climbing up. The mountain held the road close on one side but there was nothing but sky on the other. Perfect.

His fingers gently caressed the control module in anticipation. He switched on the jamming device and took control. The road was empty, save for the two escort vehicles in the front and two in the back of the truck. He pushed his virtual throttle as far as it would go and attempted to swing the truck into the other lane to bypass the escort. The truck responded, but so did the other four vehicles. The signal wasn't isolated enough to just affect the truck.

He was committed. He said a silent prayer for the soldiers in the trucks. The powerful electric motors screamed in a high-pitched protest and the tires hummed even louder. A minute went by, but it seemed like an hour to Jake. The convoy was traveling faster than any of the trucks were designed to go. The five masses vibrated violently as the tires reached their limits.

Come on. Hang in there, just a little longer! Jake pleaded.

The control module said the trucks were going one-hundred forty kilometers an hour when the road curved. The convoy followed the first truck into the guard rail like a derailed train off its tracks. It was almost graceful the way the trucks flew until they kissed the mountainside. Pieces flew, trucks bounced into the air only to hit the mountain again and again with the same result until the angry inertia laws had extracted their vengeance.

Jake hovered over the scene momentarily to take some recon pictures. He detected no survivors. Even if some of the water containers survived, the arduous terrain would make it impossible to salvage them in time.

He turned the craft toward the compound to evaluate his data. The adrenalin was still pumping when he landed, but his heart grew heavy as he and Joe and the captain analyzed the data. It showed the mangled bodies strewn over the crash site along with the water and truck debris.

The three looked on in silence. The captain, knowing all too well what Jake was feeling, scooted his chair back and put his hand on Jake's shoulder. He thought of the men he commanded in battle who didn't come back.

"Good job, soldier," he said as he walked away.

Joe stayed to support his buddy. Jake stared at the carnage for a while, hit the button to shut it off, and made eye contact with Joe as he rose to leave. Joe saw the hurt, knew the hurt, and experienced the hurt himself.

He followed Jake to his Eagle. They didn't speak but they communicated volumes. Jake needed to get home to his family, hug his wife, and sleep in the soothing, centering light.

When his sleep cycle ended, Jake sought out Elias. They needed to talk. He needed to brief Elias on what happened the previous day and find a way to keep it from happening again. It was the hand of God that there were no civilian casualties. He spotted Elias on his way to breakfast.

"Wait up Elias, I need to talk to you."

"Hey, welcome back!" Elias greeted. "How'd it go yesterday?"

He could tell that something was weighing down on Jake.

"Not so good. The software didn't discriminate between vehicles, and I took out the whole convoy."

Elias was silent. What did he overlook? he wondered. He stopped dead in his tracks.

"Of course! The military doesn't pay the satellite fees that civilians do. How could I be so stupid?"

"You mean it would tell the difference between military and civilian vehicles?" Jake asked.

"Yes, every vehicle has a code it sends to the satellite so the government can collect their user fees.

The software is supposed to single out the vehicle by that code and only jam that one. The military doesn't have that code because they don't pay for the service, so every truck in range was affected."

"That makes me feel a lot better. All I could think about last night was what if there were civilian travelers on that road."

"I've got to go back to see if another shipment is on its way to replace that one."

"I'll work on the fix for the software. They have to have some kind of code to discern between vehicles. Meanwhile, try getting closer to the target this time so the signal will be narrower."

"I'll do that. I've got to go. See you on the next trip. I'll brief you on our progress."

Jake left for the rebel compound to see if they had any news about the effectiveness of the plan.

When he arrived, Joe had already taken his men on the mission to gather ground intel. Captain Marshall was in contact with Joe and filled him in.

"So far there is no panic. The officers have kept everything under control. Another shipment is due in a few hours. No foul play is expected. Just classifies as an accident."

Jake grinned. "I guess I'll just have to change their minds about that!"

"Happy hunting, Sergeant!" Marshall said.

Jake turned and headed toward his bird. He was mulling over ways to curtail the shipments even further. Elias gave him free range with his Eagle now. He knew where the nearest bottling plant was located. Maybe he would kill every truck with the "A" logo until the idiots quit broadcasting the fact on the side of the trucks.

He was back in full military mode now. When Elias told him that civilian trucks and cars wouldn't be affected, it lifted a burden off his shoulders. It was time to go hunting.

He saw the truck pull into the truck stop and into the charging station.

Of course! Why didn't I think of this sooner! The soldiers will go into the truck stop except maybe for a guard. I'll give them a few minutes to charge and settle in to eat, and then I'll strike!

He hovered and waited. The lone sentry was being relieved for a trip to the latrine. They talked for a minute, and the first guard left. The new guard set up his perimeter track. When he was as far away from the semi, on the other side of the troop transports accompanying the big rig, Jake made his move. It had been fifteen minutes. That was enough charge for where this rig was going. He was a kilometer away and 500 meters up when he struck. The big truck ripped the charger out of its post. Sparks flew. All four transports followed like puppies after their momma. There wasn't room for them all at the same time on the road. One by one, the transports slammed into the big rigs parked in the next row.

Sorry, boys! he thought, grinning from ear to ear. *Hope your insurance is paid!*

The transports were destroyed. He glanced back a minute later, and the soldiers were running frantically after the semi they were supposed to protect.

"Explain that one to your lieutenant, Sarge!" he yelled to himself.

The truck was going back the way it came down a steep grade in the passing lane. It didn't take long for it to be going as fast as the cars in its lane. Jake laid on the horn, and they all sped up or got out of the way.

He had the final resting place picked out for the truck. Halfway down the incline was a gentle turn, but Jake's truck went straight.

He let out a big whoop and flew on by the scene. He doubled back to take pictures. Those soldiers didn't know that he just saved their lives. He felt good about this kill. Only a truck was destroyed.

He recorded everything that happened so he could train others. He was pumped. Instead of turning back, he headed toward the bottling plant.

Another truck was pulling out bound for the other side of the state.

Why not? he thought and stalked the convoy to the truck stop.

He picked his time, he picked his place, and he had his target. Same results until he destroyed five trucks in one night.

Wow! That makes me an ace! he thought to himself.

He headed back to the rebel base to check on progress and give his report. He walked in with a swagger and saluted the captain.

"Reporting back, sir. Good hunting tonight. I have changed my tactics so not a single life was lost. I also had five confirmed kills on the target!"

Jake noticed the captain didn't share his enthusiasm. He looked at him puzzled, needing to know what was wrong.

"Sergeant, I've been in many firefights, sent men into many battles, but I've never seen anything like this," the captain said. "We took the enemy without a fight a few hours ago. There were no survivors."

Jake could hear the anguish in his voice.

"The men in the camp all went mad in a matter of hours," the captain continued. "They shot their own buddies, and then themselves. Blood was everywhere. Some didn't die right away; they tore the flesh from their own faces trying to exorcise their demons. The head physician recorded the progression of the madness. He was helpless. He had a stash of Amy he kept in case his patients went in to withdrawals so he was the only one to survive. When that runs out, he's doomed.

"We sent him to the closest camp. We wanted them to know what is coming. Joe is there with his men cleaning up and burying the dead. I've never seen such total devastation of a unit in my life.

"I don't know where you are in your spiritual walk, sir, but the Bible is full of stories where God has shown his power. He once took three-hundred men and defeated a nation. He commanded the Israelites to totally destroy the nations before them, and the times they disobeyed have hindered their progress to this day. Read the Bible, it's all in there. God is at work here," Jake admonished.

"I've got work to do," Jake said as he left the room. He left the captain to ponder over his words.

Jake couldn't un-see the images on the captain's screen. He shuddered at the fact that the insurgence had just begun. It was a matter of time before the enemy regrouped and struck back with a vengeance. His methods had to be shared with Edens across the world, so they could protect the refugees in their part of the world. Jake had to get back to report to Elias.

He found Elias in his lab poring over the data Jake provided. Elias had a tired smile. He'd been up all sleep cycle to try and fix the flaw in his system.

He greeted Jake with a man-shake and set back down at his computer.

"I think I've figured out what to do about the military trucks. It seems the software is the same as any truck but the tracking has been disabled. I'm working on a program to activate that code now."

"Don't fret, my friend," Jake chided. "Ole Jake pulled your butt out of the fire again!" I worked around the flaw and got five kills this trip."

"Seriously, we need to get this to the rest of Edens all over the world. When you finish the software, you should ramp up the production of these devices. The NWO won't stand by and let a bunch of people they deem disposable riff-raffs take control of their outposts at will forever," continued Jake.

"You mean....?"

"Yeah, I mean. The pictures are graphic and disturbing, but every soldier except one died mostly by his own hands. That drug is the most controlling, soul-destroying thing this world has ever seen. We took the weapon the Beast used to take control and turned it against them. I see a God thing myself! He destroyed these soldiers just like he did the Philistine when David threw his rock.

"There is no humanity, or dignity, or even valor in this army. I think if we can strike hard and fast, these people will turn tail and run to the nearest bottled water stand and defend the Amy supply regardless what the NWO commanders say.

"I'll get the production started. We have the basic controls. It's off the shelf stuff, and the software is open sourced so anyone can use it; we just need to get them installed and distributed. Get as many ready as you can. I'll start training and distribution after I catch some shuteye."

Elias and his team loaded the new system onto the forklifts and started toward the birds.

Elias's team was loading Jakes bird when he walked in.

"I've got twenty of them ready. We have instructions on how to reproduce the devices in each one."

"Came through once again."

"Did you expect anything less?"

"No, I didn't. You seem to have a knack for doing the impossible right on schedule," Jake said. "Now, stand back and let a marine save the day!"

"Glory hound!" Elias accused with a grin.

"Yep!"

With that, Jake walked up his ramp to free the rebels, wherever they were on the planet.

34

Nuclear Veagence?

Chione, the generals, and the Beast were all there at the summit. The news was not good. It seemed the whole NWO forces were in full retreat. The fear and the reality of losing the access to the water outweighed any loyalty to the cause. All over the world, the tiny rebel forces were mocking the best-equipped, largest military entity that had ever existed.

Gustaf, still the head of security, was in attendance. He listened as the Beast took control of the meeting.

The Beast had recovered from his external wounds, but Gustaf knew he was a shadow of his former self. He was prone to debilitating headaches and would lash out at anyone he could reach. Gustaf steered clear of him whenever possible. The Beast's stamina was low, and after a few minutes, he would have to leave the meeting. The Beast rose to the podium.

"There is only one solution to this insubordination," the Beast said. "Total annihilation! The American cities will be bombed and brought to ruble. We have enough nuclear weapons to lay waste to it all. They started this rebel movement, but we are going to end it!"

Gustaf rose slightly out of his seat. "But Your Excellency, I thought we... Got ...rid of... all?" His voice trailed off at the Beast's withering glare.

Of course, they wouldn't get rid of them. They would just confiscate them. The thought flashed through the back of his mind as he sat down in silence.

This is pure madness! The people in those cities were ninety-nine percent loyal subjects with the mark. Thought Gustaf.

It seemed like the cowardly way out to him. Instead of going after the real enemy, they were going after soft targets. He should have protested against this plan, but he took out his flask and took a sip instead. Everyone else stood silent as well.

The Beast stormed out of the summit. His face was red, and his head pounded with the exertion. Everybody around him was an incompetent imbecile. Why did he have to solve all the world's problems?

He had a lot of time to reflect on his journey back to health. His master and father Satan was able to restore fully his part of the brain, but most of the human side withered. He always thought his father's genes gave him the desire and the ability to squeeze the essences of fear and death he so craved from his victims; the evil acts that made his life bearable.

Could it be his human side unleashed, barren of goodness, isolated from its creator, gave him those abilities? He pondered over all of this as he popped another pain pill.

The generals talked among themselves about the coming holocaust. The nuclear power unleashed on every city in the US would cause a nuclear winter in most of the world, not to mention the fallout that would drift throughout the earth. The Beast didn't seem to know or care about what happened to anyone since his resurrection. They had to talk some reason into him.

They all knew of Gustaf's loyalty and his precarious position with Chione. They unanimously appointed him to talk to the Beast and convince him to rethink his position on the nuclear weapons. He was in no position to decline the assignment.

The cowards, he thought to himself as he listened to his assignment.

They knew as well as he that this was a death warrant. They got their courage out of the same bottle he did. But there was a difference. He was still a soldier. If he was to die, at least it would be in the line of duty, at the hands of the one he served, carrying out orders.

He put his affairs in order. The next day when he went for his morning briefing, he would bring up the subject. Maybe the Beast would be in a more receptive mood after he slept.

Gustaf knocked on his door mid-morning, after the Beast's drug affects began to wane, as he usually did. While waiting, he absentmindedly took out his water flask to take a hit for his nerves. He looked at the flask for a minute, wondering how his life would have been without his dependence. Then he threw it as hard as he could. It made a loud clattering exit as it careened down the hall.

"Come in," he heard from within. He swallowed hard and entered. The Beast was sitting on his throne in his private quarters, rubbing his forehead from the drugs and the pain. His eyes stayed closed. He knew it was Gustaf. He came every day at this time.

"Here is the completed list of tasks from yesterday, Your Highness."

"Put them on the table, Gustaf, next to your assignments for today. Take them with you."

This was normally the extent of their exchange every morning. Instead of bowing and leaving, Gustaf stood his ground. The Beast opened his eyes and stared at Gustaf.

"Is there something else?" The Beast glared; his bloodshot eyes fixed on Gustaf.

"Yes, Your Highness," Gustaf declared, standing at attention. "I have a list of all the negative effects of using nuclear weapons on the scale that would be needed to take out every city in America. The council and I would ask that you reconsider."

I hope he is swift, Gustaf thought.

Almost before the words crossed his mind, the Beast was upon him. It was futile to resist. Even in his weakened state, the Beast had the power of a large grizzly bear. Gustaf died instantly, with dignity. The Beast looked at the severed head of his minion for a moment. Was that remorse? No, he was thinking how hard it would be to replace his servant. He tossed Gustaf's head on the heap that was his body.

It's useless to torture them anymore, I can no longer feel the essence of fear I needed, the Beast thought as the skull landed on the heap.

He sat back down on his throne and went back to massaging his forehead. He finally rose and paced the room slowly. He stopped in front of a full-length mirror in the hall. He peered at his face. It was symmetrical, and the scars were covered by expert cosmetologists when he went out in public. If only his brain would heal. His hatred for Christians boiled. He was about ready to rip the mirror from the wall when Chione entered.

She was the only one the Beast gave total access to his life. She saw Gustaf's remains and recruited some orderlies to remove them.

I guess the generals had their answer, she thought.

"We are preparing the next speech at the sacrifice ceremony set for this weekend," she said. "We will need to have you make a brief appearance at the start. Are you up to it?"

"Yes, of course," he answered sullenly.

"Here is the script for the event. We will proceed with the plans to make an example of the American insolence. We will need time to redirect the missiles and pick our targets."

He only nodded.

"In one month, the country will no longer exist. All life will be destroyed." Her comments were designed to get some reaction from him, but he sat motionless, and emotionless.

I want him to rule the world, not destroy it, she thought as she walked out of his chambers with a heavy heart.

She ordered the immediate evacuation of all forces stationed in the North American continent. Although Canada and Mexico were not targeted, fallout would make portions of those countries uninhabitable.

All military ships, transport planes, trains, and buses were pressed into service for the military evacuation. Every military base was abandoned.

35

Calm Before the Storm

Captain Marshal couldn't believe his intel. The rebels were advancing as fast as their new pilfered military equipment would take them. Roads were blocked, and strategic bridges blown up, but no army opposed them. They were getting confident, and downright cocky.

Instead of being elated, he felt disturbed. He did a lot of pacing, and thinking. Why would a well-equipped army not take a stand? His gut instinct told him he needed answers.

Jake had been making regular runs back to Eden with new converts. He was elated to be carrying God's people once again. The captain put out word that he needed to see him the next trip.

Jake strolled in a few hours later, with the arrogance of a Top Gun pilot.

"You wanted to see me, sir?"

"Yes, yes. I need you to gather me some intel on their troop movements. I want to know why they're not putting up any struggle. This just isn't right."

"Relax, Captain. They've turned tail and ran like the cowards they are."

"This is something different. I know their chain of command has never been tested but I thought they would regroup and come at us. They're just leaving. I need to know the extent of the withdrawal, and the reason.

"Okay, Captain, but I think you're being a little paranoid."

"Humor me, Sergeant."

"Yes, sir. I'll leave after I have the last group safely in Eden.

Jake got his load safely to their destination and took off. He stalked every known military install-ment he could think of. The intel was the same. They were all leaving in a hurry. Big ships were docking from every former nation in the world. The flags were NWO but they came from Russia, China, and the UK, everywhere. Jake didn't know why, but he knew how. He wasn't sure what the captain was after, so he recorded everything.

He saw the missile by chance. In his travels to and from each coast, he stumbled on a large truck car-rying a huge intercontinental ballistic missile. The convoy wasn't trying to be discreet, or clandestine.

The markings on the missile were clear. They carried nuclear warheads.

Jake told himself that they were just part of the effort to destroy all nuclear weapons like the Beast promised when taking over, but his instinct told him different. He changed his priority to the middle of Kansas flatlands and Minnesota corn fields. He saw in his youth many documentaries of the missile silos that existed just under camouflaged bunkers in the middle of nowhere manned in secret by android soldiers. Those were mainly propaganda films put out by the government. He crisscrossed the nation filling in the grid on his system. When he finished his mission, he returned to the captain.

The captain noticed right away the change in Jake's swagger. Jake didn't have his usual banter. He just jumped into his briefing.

"I noticed that all military personnel are leaving," Jake said. "They are not leaving because of us. They are leaving because they are being evacuated. Something big is going down and I stumbled on it by accident.

"I saw a very large, Russian-style carrier with an intercontinental missile strapped to it. They weren't making any attempt to hide. I thought at first it was part of the effort to do away with all nuclear weapons, like the Beast promised when he took over, but something wasn't right.

"I mapped the grid, mainly in the mid-west, and upper mid-west. I found open silos everywhere.

They weren't dismantling the missiles; they were maintaining them! I've caught what you got, Captain."

They sat in silence, not knowing what to say.

"We don't say anything to anybody until we verify this stuff," the captain finally spoke. "We don't want to make a mistake about this. Worldwide panic would be devastating. We don't know who is targeted, whether it is one city or a whole state, or worse case, the whole country. We are dealing with a mad man, so logic is out the window."

"I know some generals that are still active; one of them was at the summit. I need to make a road trip. Could you drop me off in DC? I have some catching up to do."

"Sure, Captain. I can get you there in an hour if you don't mind the g-force."

"I'll meet you in the landing area in ten minutes."

Jake went about readying for flight. He wasn't sure where or how, but he would get Captain Marshall where he wanted to go. He was a little worried about all the security in the DC area. The captain strolled in and they lifted off.

"Do you have a specific location, Captain?"

"General Whorley and I go way back. He was the only one to testify in my defense at my court martial. It cost him a star, but he knows the politics of the military. I think he had the goods on somebody because he recovered quickly. He's got a favorite watering hole we used to go to. Drop me there. Here's the address."

"Yes, sir!"

Jake was relieved he didn't say the Pentagon. He didn't think even his security could get in there.

Jake dropped off the captain and went about his business delivering more and more converts to Eden, but with a heavy heart. He couldn't help but run different scenarios through his mind about the coming holocaust. He wondered at times if it was futile to take these converts to Eden. What if the fallout reached there?

He spoke only when someone spoke to him and sometimes not even then. His only respite was the sleep cycles and his family. He wished he had someone he could share with but he'd given the captain his word. Until this was a certainty, he wouldn't even confide in Elias.

It was the longest three days he ever experienced. He was at the rendezvous point early in anticipation. The captain walked up the ramp. Jake couldn't help himself. He laughed out loud.

The captain was sporting a black eye, and his lower lip didn't close.

"What happened, Captain? You get mugged?"

"Had a little difference of opinion on whose turn it was to buy," he replied with as much of a grin as his swollen lip would allow.

"Ain't the half of it. Four-star General Whorley has to report for duty tomorrow sporting a broken nose and two black eyes. He told me everything. He was dying to tell someone, and he knew I was someone who needed to know.

"He also said that the inner circle is considering sabotage. The missiles would go off, miss their marks, and land in the ocean or the desert. He flat out told me the Beast has lost all ability to govern since the he was shot. We need to prepare for the worse and hope for the best."

"Captain, you can hope all you want; me," Jake said. "I'm gonna pray!"

"Yeah, that too."

They flew the rest of the way to the compound in silence. When they landed, Jake reached in his pocket and handed captain a silicone paper.

"You've been around Joe and me enough to know our faith. Keep that paper with you. If you ever feel the presence of God and accept Jesus, just take out that paper. If you see Jesus on the Cross, we'll know and come and get you."

The captain took it out of respect. He couldn't see himself ever needing it, or using it.

Jake went to his designated rendezvous to ferry a load of converts to Eden. He couldn't wait to brief Elias on his findings. He went straight to Elias when he landed.

"I've got some really bad news. The NWO has plans to destroy the whole continent with nuclear bombs. The Beast has a vendetta against us for showing his troops the way home. What are we going to do, Elias? We can't stand by and wait for the end!" Jake paced back and forth, beside himself with anxiety. "Even if we don't take a direct hit, the radiation will wipe us out!"

Elias watched him and let him vent for a few minutes. The calmer Elias seemed; the more agitated Jake became.

"Don't you get it, man? We're gonna die a horrible death and there's nothing we can do!"

Elias caught him by the forearm and looked him straight in the eye. "Jake, Jake, Jake! We are not alone. Gods got this!"

Jake remembered saying nearly the same thing to Joe a few days ago. He calmed down.

"Did you ever wonder why we don't have day and night here?" Elias asked. "Why we don't feel the seasonal change here? Why we can't be seen when you enter and exit?"

"Yeah, I've often wondered about that," Jake answered.

"When you are here, you are on God's time. The Eagles are able to travel freely in both realms because they use the energy that God provided for us, but we rejected, in favor of fossil fuels. It is the only thing available in both worlds. It's the only thing that will be left when Jesus returns to the new world. Don't you see, Jake? We are already in the new world!"

"When the Tribulation is over, we will live freely on the earth with the rightful heir on the throne."

Jake pondered over Elias's words.

"You mean all the trips I've made I've been traveling through time?"

"Yep!"

Jake felt like the weight of the world was lifted from his shoulders. But his elation was short lived. His face clouded.

"What about the ones left behind?"

"We have done everything the Lord has asked," Elias said softly, solemnly. "Their fate is up to God in his mercy. Noah's Ark had to close to the world at some point in time."

"We can only pray."

Jake just stared into space for a long time. Elias sat with him. Finally, Elias spoke.

"Why don't we pray for the captain. That's all we can do."

They both got on their knees and prayed earnestly for the captain. When they were satisfied they had prayed to fulfillment, they both rose.

Jake patted Elias on the shoulder as he passed him to leave. Jake's heart was still burdened but he felt he had done all he could. It was now up to God.

Jake was exhausted. The kind of tired that comes with thinking that he'd done his best and still failed. The captain saved millions of souls but was in danger of losing his own. Jake never felt this burdened for a soul in his live.

The door to his part of Eden came into view. Maybe the sleep cycle would revive him he thought, it has always worked before.

He placed his palm on the door and entered. *Maybe a hot shower would help calm my soul and help me sleep,* he thought. Even as the water cascaded down his face he prayed. Never before had he prayed so earnestly for another.

Instead of getting in bed he knelt beside it, rocking like a Haredi Jew at the wailing wall, his soul still in anguish.

"Lord, hear my prayer for my lost brother!" he wailed.

Jake could feel the battle for the soul of his comrade on that distant mountain. He was deep in prayer until he heard a pounding on his door.

Annoyed by the interruption he got up to answer.

Elias didn't greet him; he couldn't talk for the emotion welling within. He thrust the paper at Jake and grinned. He'd given thousands of flight logs to Jake over their time in the Eden but this one was special to both of them.

"Couldn't this wait. It isn't my rotation on the flight deck yet." Jake said.

Elias held out the paper again and pointed to the coordinates.

"Look at the location!"

He stared at the paper. It took a minute for Jake to understand.

"You mean...?"

"Yeah, the captain. Who else do you know that lives that high on that Mountain?"

Jake let out a whoop that shook the room, picked Elias up in a bear hug and danced him around the room. He deposited Elias in a chair and with flight plan in hand disappeared into his bedroom.

Elias smiled at the exuberance of his old friend and mentor. Elias was never a marine but he fought in the Lord's Army and understood the bond formed from going through the fire of adversity together. The tougher the times, the stronger the bond.

Jake dressed hurriedly.

"I got somewhere to go. I'll meet you on the flight deck."

Elias acknowledged him as he ran out the door. Elias showed himself out and shut the door. He caught a glimpse of Jake running in the direction of Joe's quarters.

"Hey Joe, wake up!" Jake barked as he pounded on Joe's door.

After what seemed to Jake an eternity the door opened. Joe stood there with eyes not fully opened.

"Get dressed Joe, I need some help. We gotta go rescue the captain."

He didn't really need the help but he knew what the captain meant to Joe and wanted him in on the airlift.

Joe finally realized what Jake was saying and double timed back to his bedroom to get his clothes. He came out of his room dressing on the way. He tucked in his shirt on the way through the door.

After the captain's attitude when they saw him last, Joe was still in disbelief but he wouldn't miss this for the world.

Jake's Eagle sat ready on the flight deck when they entered the area. Elias was standing at the ramp to see them off.

"Bring him home brothers!" he said as they hurried up the steps, "Your bird is good to go."

36

The Rescued Warrior

Jake started his flight check before he even sat down. The ramp raised with the familiar whoosh. The seal allowed the cabin to pressurize. Joe found his seat and buckled in as the landing gear retracted and the bird took flight.

The exhilaration of flight coupled with the mission overwhelmed Jake.

Yehaaaaaaaaay!" he yelped, pumping his fist in the air.

Joe answered with a marine, "Ooray!"

Pure joy was tempered only by the logistics of the mission. Jake focused on the mission and the coordinates.

When they closed in on the location, Jake took manual control and hunted for the right spot to settle in. He was unprepared for what he saw when the captain came into view.

The captain was sitting on a flat rock with his feet barely touching the ground. His arms were locked at the elbow, palms down, propping up his torso. The silicon paper was opened, lying on the rock glistening in the morning Colorado sun. He looked totally spent.

"Hey, Joe, come and look at this."

"What do we do now?" Joe asked.

There in front of the captain was the biggest grizzly that either had ever seen. It was setting on its backside facing the captain with its nose centimeters away from his. It was as still as a statue.

"What do we do know?" asked Joe again.

"I bet that's old Marley's grizzly." He said out loud to himself.

"Huh?" Jake inquired puzzled.

"Long story. Part of the captain's lore I heard while tracking him. I'll tell you someday. You didn't happen to bring any weapons, did you?" Asked Joe.

"I've never needed weapons to rescue any of my passengers from a bear before." Replied Jake.

"What do we do now?" asked Joe.

They fell silent, analyzing the situation, when Jake poked Joe's arm.

"Did you see that?" he said.

"See what?" Joe inquired, looking at the screen intently.

"The captain motioned us to come to him," said Jake.

"But there's a bear there!" replied Joe incredulously.

When the captain waved, the bear got on all fours and turned to analyze the intruders. He sniffed the air until he was satisfied he was in control of the situation, sauntered a few meters away from the captain, turned facing the path the intruders had to use to get to the captain, and plopped on his backside. His position assured him that nothing could transpire without his approval.

Jake started to lower the bay door, watching it intently as it turned in to the stairway.

"What are you doing! There's a bear down there! Do you know how fast those things can run?" Joe exclaimed.

"Calm down, Joe. That bear means us no harm. If he did, he would have already killed the captain. This is what we are going to do; We're going to walk down the ramp slow and steady, no sudden moves, no eye contact with the bear. Walk straight to the captain and put your arm under his armpit and slowly lift him to his feet. Then we're going to walk back up the ramp with him."

"I suppose I get the side closest to the bear?" Joe stammered.

He was still terrified of that bear.

"Of course, Joe, you know the old saying, "I don't have to outrun the bear, I just have to outrun you!"" Jake answered him with mischief in his eyes.

"There's something peculiar about that bear's behavior, Joe. Grizzly's don't like people. A normal bear would have killed the captain and left. This one actually looks like it is protecting him."

He was willing to risk his and Joe's life on his hunch.

Joe reluctantly matched Jake's stride down the ramp. In his peripheral vision he could see the bear watching their every move. He could hear a muffled grunt every time the bear breathed. Nature would call it to hibernation soon and judging from its girth it had been very successful packing on the kilograms in preparation.

As soon as they were safely inside the Eagle, Jake hit the button to raise the ramp. Joe breathed a sigh of relief when it fully closed. Jake programmed the bird for flight while Joe buckled the captain in.

Just before the ramp closed completely, they all heard a roar emanating from the bear that shook the mountain. On the monitor they saw he was on his hind legs with his claws bared high in the air. They knew he was letting them know who ruled the mountain and that they were no longer welcome.

The Eagle took flight as the bear turned and disappeared into the trees. The captain was going home.

. . .

The captain was so exhausted he slept the whole journey. At Jake's request there was a stretcher waiting to take the captain to the infirmary so he could be evaluated. He looked like he'd been in a fight with that grizzly.

The captain woke as they were loading him on the stretcher, "Men, have I got a story for you! You probably won't believe it but I need to tell someone while its fresh in my mind."

"You just rest for now. Tomorrow Joe and I will look you up and listen to what you have to say," said Jake, "right now Joe and I need some shuteye too."

He watched as they wheeled the captain into the infirmary. The exhaustion of the rescue overwhelmed him.

He looked at Joe. Without saying a thing, they started back to their own quarters. Mission accomplished. They would both sleep good for the remainder of the sleep cycle.

37

Safe Haven

The captain opened his eyes. His pristine surroundings were unfamiliar to him. It took a minute for his puzzled mind to catch his reality.

I remember Joe and Jake hustling me up the stairs to a seat in Jake's Eagle and landing in this place, but I don't know what this place is? Joe thought.

He felt strong enough to sit up in bed.

"Owwwhh," escaped from his lips as he sat up.

Every muscle in his body hurt and he was a little woozy.

"Anybody here?" he yelled when he stabilized.

A nurse came in and greeted him.

"How are you this morning captain?" she greeted while checking him out.

She took blood pressure, oxygen level, pulse, looked into his pupils, and checked over his many scrapes, bruises, and contusions.

"I'd be better if you would tell me where I am?"

"You're in an Eden. You were brought in at the beginning of the sleep cycle by Jake and Joe in an Eagle."

"So, it wasn't a dream?" he asked.

She smiled and answered, "no, it's not a dream."

"Would you like something to eat, captain?"

"Yes, Mam, I'd like that very much. I haven't eaten in a long time."

She brought him a plate piled high with something he didn't recognize but he was hungry enough to eat almost anything. He took a bite and closed his eyes in ecstasy.

"What is this stuff?" he asked.

"We don't really know," said the nurse, "it's something that God provides for those that have had a rough time getting here. We just call it Manna. It only shows up when there is a need. Enjoy, you will probably never have it again."

The captain did just that. He savored every bite, washing it down with the hot coffee the nurse provided. He could feel his strength returning. He was finishing when Joe and Jake sauntered into the room.

"How are you feeling today, captain?" asked Jake.

"A lot better than last night," he replied.

"You're looking a lot stronger. You were really out of it last night." Joe chimed in.

They weren't there for a social call; they were both dying to hear the captain's story. They fell silent and waited for the captain to speak.

"Well, looks like I'm up," said the captain.

He continued as Joe and Jake got comfortable in the chairs the infirmary provided.

"I was hunting for some food. I'd let my supplies get too low. I was almost out of any kind of meat. I didn't have any luck hunting that night. When that old grizzly is on my, or should I say his side of the mountain, the critters scatter for a safer place. I was almost home when I saw this thing that looked like a lamb in the pathway. It was a pathetic looking creature; looking like someone had already killed it but it wouldn't die."

"I reached for it and it turned into a lion and knocked me flat on my back and pinned me to the ground."

"This is the crazy part. I thought that lion was talking to me. It kept saying

"Surrender Montgomery Marshal."

"Every time it said that it vanished and let me up. Then I thought I was fighting a man but I saw wings on his back. It was all so surreal. I thought I was dreaming."

Marshal continued, "you men know I don't surrender. Just when I thought I was going to get the best of that being I was fighting, that lion would come back, pin me down and say again, "Surrender Montgomery Marshal" and I'd fight that much harder."

"This went on most of the night until I was completely spent. That Lion Pinned me down and said again, "surrender to me". I had nothing left. I wondered what was after me and why."

"I laid there flat on my back wondering if this was the way my life would end, torn apart by a lion. For the first time in my life, I didn't have any fight left and I was out of options. That lion just stared at me and for the first time I looked into its eyes."

"Its face seemed to glow and I saw only love and compassion, not the triumph of a conquering beast. I shut my eyes and finally surrendered for the first time in my life. I couldn't hold back the tears. They ran down the side of my face to the soil below me."

"I was taken back to the court martial. I relived every lie and false testimony brought against me. I had to endure the ceremony that stripped away my commission and drummed me out of the core over again. I couldn't believe that the country I served, watch soldiers die for, and killed for......would do such a thing to me," he said with a faltering voice.

He fell silent for a moment, then continued, "When my eyes opened again the dawn was just breaking. When I focused, I saw that old grizzly! It wasn't a lion like I thought, it was that bear!"

"He had me pinned down with his hind legs on mine and his front paws pinning my arms. It was strange, he wasn't hurting me at all. He had his nose almost touching mine. He had the same compassionate eyes I saw the night before in the lion. His breath smelled sweet like honey. It seemed that with every breath that bear took some of the bitterness, anger, and pain left my body."

"I had no option but to relax and let him work. He finally moved to one side. I was so weak I couldn't move so he nudged me with his nose until I rolled over and then he offered his head to give me something to hold onto. I finally made it to the flat rock and sat down. That old bear sat right in front of me on his backside like a statue."

"I felt cleansed, empty, like a painter's canvass. I raised my head and said yes. The sun crested the mountain ridge as the Son entered my heart. I've seen thousands of sunrises on that mountain sitting on that same rock but none of them can compare to the one I just witnessed!"

"That bear nudged my pocket where the silicon paper you gave me was so I took in out. When I touched it, the most beautiful picture of our Lord and savior appeared and here I am."

The captain fell silent. Everyone in the infirmary was silent, they had all paused to listen to the captain's testimony. Joe and Jake sat spellbound. When they were sure he was done they went over to him and shook his hand, hugged him, and welcomed him to the family of God.

38

Satan's Revenge

He came out of the sea the day after the tsunami subsided. Those that saw him claimed his scaly skin was never wetted from the sea. The water never touched his body. The red heat of his being prevented it. He was flung from the heavens in a time known to God only, never to return.

Another beast appeared from across the land. He took all the worst demons to his person as he passed by. He had a rendezvous with his master Satan and his cohort Nicholas.

Chaos and panic followed in their wake. No beasts had ever been seen on the face of the earth like these two. All who saw them saw different images—all sinister, fear mongering images of the Hades yet to come, they entered the chambers of Nicholas, unannounced.

He felt their presence but didn't look up. He knew who they were instinctively.

"What do you want?"

Before he could take another breath, the beast from the sea picked him off of his throne without touching him and threw him across the room into the wall with so much force the Temple shook. Nicholas lunged at the beast but was caught in mid-lunge and suspended. Nicholas' throat began tightening until he could no longer breath. For the first time in his life, he knew the fear that he savored from others. The Beast's face was so close that Nicholas felt the hot stench of his words in his face. Nicholas' scars burned red. He was slammed onto his throne with such force that the base cracked.

"I'll teach you to show respect for your Father!"

Nicholas's head pounded more than usual from the exertion.

"What do you want, my Lord?" he said without looking up.

"You pathetic idiot! I give you the world and you can't keep order. Your showboating carelessness nearly cost you your life and me dominance over the entire world. I've been planning this since my fall. Now you're going to destroy half the world because of your inability to control a handful of peasants on a mountain!"

The scales on Satan's body glowed red!

"You don't have a clue, do you? My power lies in the numbers. I am nothing without humankind. I destroy, not create! They are my leverage, my only weapon against their Creator. When they cease to exist, I cease to exist! They are my breeding stock, my one chance at immortality, my reason to exist, and you want to destroy them! I will use them to maximize the impact of my evil in the presence of God starting with the Jews! The timing is not right yet. Watch and learn, imbecile!"

He was pacing back and forth in front of Nicholas, making sure to make eye contact. Nicholas had to look away; he melted with fear at the powerful evil that was his father.

The beast continued, "From now on, you are just a pretty face, a figurehead just like your golden likeness in front of the Temple. I will tell you what to say and when to say it. Your counterpart will be my enforcer, my eyes and ears.

"We will say that an attempt at overthrowing the NWO resulted in some nuclear warheads that had not been destroyed yet falling into the wrong hands, but the courageous efforts of the Beast thwarted the military coup before innocent lives were lost."

Nickolas sat sullen, silent, like an adolescent child caught in the act, repentant only because he was being punished.

"Since you're in charge now, get rid of the two who are preaching the Word of the God of Abraham outside my window day and night! The crowds are getting out of hand and they are convincing these Jews to follow Jesus."

"I offered a generous reward to anyone that killed them, but anyone going near to them with the in-tent to harm those two ends up burned to death by the flames from their mouths. It hasn't rained for a month, and all the crops are withered and dried just because they shut off the clouds."

"I ordered the troops to fire randomly into the crowd to disperse it, killing hundreds, but the next day they were back like moths drown to flame. They refuse the mark and refuse to bow to me or my image. I have beheaded multitudes until the blood splattered as high as the bridles of a horse, still they come!

"Boils and open sores have erupted on the skin of anyone who has the mark. The moaning and cursing keep me up at night. It is all driving me mad!"

"Nicholas ended his tirade and massaged his head with both hands trying to ease the pain his father couldn't heal him from.

In the back of his mind, Nicholas remembered the words he read in the last book of the Bible in his childhood. He dismissed them as fantasy, something to scare the followers into following the worthless God of Abraham. Now he was tormented by the knowledge. He seemed to know what was going to happen and when. A Prophet in his own doom!

39

End Times Approach

Jake landed in Eden with the last load of missionaries pulled back when the news of the coming holocaust spread. He had one last convert with him. It was the eleventh hour. The gates of salvation were fast closing, and the gates of hell were open wide. He was exhausted from the stress and urgency of getting all believers back in the fold. He was going to take a good long soak in his tub and relax at home for this sleep cycle.

There were more people out there he was sure, but he was too tired to be of any good to anyone.

Elias greeted him, "Good job, my friend!"

Elias always wanted a debriefing when he got in but he was just too tired. He put his hand on Elias' shoulder and looked him in the eye. Elias nodded.

He'd been that half-dead exhausted many times. Jake walked away without a word and Elias let him.

The next cycle, like he had done every working day of his life, Jake got up to leave, kissed his wife goodbye, and headed to the debriefing and break-fast before heading out on his next adventure. His life had been legendary since he signed on with Elias to fly the Eagles. He thanked God every day for the privilege to be part of his kingdom.

Elias broke the news after breakfast. The Eagles were grounded.

"What do you mean, the Eagles are ground-ed!" Jake nearly spat out his last swallow of coffee. "There're still people there! We can't stop now!"

Elias spoke, "All of you in this room who piloted the Eagles are to be congratulated on a job well done. I agree with Jake. There are still those left behind, but it is up to their creator now whether they survive the Tribulation."

"Come on, Elias. Just one more time! Please."

"You don't understand, Jake. We didn't ground the Eagles on some sort of whim. They have ceased to function. The energy that they need is gone. They won't fly. God has closed the door of the Ark. We are in the Tribulation. We are no longer safe out there. The day of repentance is past.

"We are in God's hands and in his time. A day is a lifetime, and a lifetime a day. All I can say is come, Lord Jesus, come."

Hate is not the opposite of love. Hate is twin to love, both born out of passion and separated only by the one chromosome called perception. The Beast's greatest weapon was the ability to manipulate that perception. The opposite of love is fear. Fear creates hate out of love.

Nicholas was incapable of love or compassion. His actions were governed by the need for humans to fear him. It gave him total control. He used it to manipulate the mind, pervert morals, and ultimately control the destiny of humanity.

Thank You

Thank you for reading my book. If you enjoyed it, please take a moment to leave me a review.

About Author

The author lives in Indiana with his wife of fifty years Suzanne. Together they raised four daughters and are in the process of spoiling three grandchildren. Daniel likes to garden and enjoys sharing his delicious sweet corn every season with neighbors and friends. He has been to Cuba with Living In Faith ministries installing water systems and distributing Bibles to the churches. It has become his passion to get Bibles to the Cuban churches.

In his retirement he likes to write novels and short stories. To enjoy his stories and connect directly with Dan, visit daniellfultonwritingforyou.com.

www.ingramcontent.com/pod-product-compliance
Lightning Source LLC
Chambersburg PA
CBHW061231310726
48971CB00007B/2022